A ROOF AGAINST THE RAIN

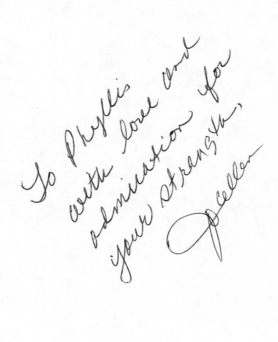

A ROOF AGAINST THE RAIN

A Novel

JoEllen Collins

iUniverse, Inc.

New York Bloomington Shanghai

A ROOF AGAINST THE RAIN

iUniverse books may be ordered through booksellers or by contacting:

iUniverse
1663 Liberty Drive
Bloomington, IN 47403
www.iuniverse.com
1-800-Authors (1-800-288-4677)

Because of the dynamic nature of the Internet, any Web addresses or links contained in this book may have changed since publication and may no longer be valid.

This is a work of fiction. All of the characters, names, incidents, organizations, and dialogue in this novel are either the products of the author's imagination or are used fictitiously.

ISBN: 978-0-595-51720-6 (pbk)
ISBN: 978-0-595-62005-0 (ebk)

Printed in the United States of America

For my daughters

Sonnet XXX
by
Edna St Vincent Millay

Love is not all: it is not meat nor drink
Nor slumber nor a roof against the rain
Nor yet a floating spar to men that sink
And rise and sink and rise again;
Love can not fill the thickened lung with breath,
Nor clean the blood, nor set the fractured bone;
Yet many a man is making friends with death
Even as I speak, for lack of love alone.
It well may be that in a difficult hour,
Pinned down by pain and moaning for release,
Or nagged by want past resolution's power,
I might be driven to sell your love for peace,
Or trade the memory of this night for food.
It well may be. I do not think I would.

CHAPTER 1

▼

She just wanted to get the job done, get the condo cleared out for the renters, get all the leftover bits and fluffs of their life together put away somewhere safe. It was proving harder than she planned.

When Oliver Simms told her he'd found a rental for the upcoming Christmas season, she'd reacted with relief, the most positive feeling she'd been able to muster so close to Paul's death. She really hadn't wanted to spend Christmas in Sun Valley anyway; trying to recreate past family ski vacations was going to be impossible without Paul there. Perhaps next year she would feel up to having the girls for a Sun Valley Christmas again. But not this season. And since she had the luxury of some free time for the first time in recent memory, she had planned to come up to their vacation home now, in the fall, instead of then. She wanted to be here when the leaves fell, take some long and ruminating walks, see some of the good friends they'd gathered over the years, and use the gaps between social obligations to sort through the things still left from Paul.

Paul … the THINGS! Getting rid of so many things! The idea of throwing away Paul's possessions seemed callous, but it had to be done. Each item she picked up and discarded or passed on would bring some pain, she knew. Once she cleared through the physical remnants of her years with Paul, the intangibles would always be there. She would still be able to hear his laugh echoing in the empty rooms he'd once filled and treasure his spirit of grabbing on to life.

Even now she could thank that exuberance: in spite of her reticence, he had insisted that they indulge in a second home in Idaho when the girls were small and she was teaching in Santa Monica. He convinced her it was a legacy they could enjoy way before it would ever be bequeathed.

And he'd been right, once again. She put her caution aside, and they began house hunting one spring break 18 years ago. She fell in love with every place they saw, thought she could make the homes theirs with just a touch of paint or cutting out an extra window or adding a skylight. She remembered being enamored with a dark log cabin close enough to the ski mountain that it was shaded almost all the time. The savvy real estate agent had shown it to them on a very sunny morning. Even then the light was limited, but the smell of wood and the large fireplace had won her over. Fortunately she and Paul returned at twilight and realized that the place was too small and dark. Eventually they had settled on a large, new three-bedroom-and-loft condo in Elkhorn, adjacent to the beginner's ski area and convenient for their lifestyle.

It took her a few years to like this place as much as she did now. She had to admit that Paul's assumptions about its wearability had been correct. With her own decorating and by haunting antique shows and crafts fairs, it had acquired almost as much charm as the log cabin. And it was much easier to arrive on a vacation to a condo where driveways were ploughed and paths shoveled as a matter of course. Over the years she had come to love the place, finally this past year, in spite of Paul's illness, replacing the rust-colored shag carpet with wood floors and area rugs.

So she was here again, re-ordering the possessions she had shared with Paul. She procrastinated a bit, fixed herself a single cup of coffee with the cone filter Paul had given her a couple of years ago. He couldn't drink coffee anymore, but knew she loved it. The smell of the hot water dripping through the filter was reassuring. Some small pleasures remained no matter what.

She sat down on one of the pine shaker stools at the counter separating the kitchen from the dining area, added some Equal to the cup, stirred the hot coffee, and looked out the window at the golden yellow aspens turning in the early fall.

A California girl, she had always craved the sense of changing seasons. While people watching the Rose Parade on television dreamed of moving out West where the weather was temperate, she planned to attend college somewhere where she could crunch leaves in October. She laughed now as she thought of her eventual choice: UCLA, about as un-Eastern as one could get. The substitute for dry fall leaves had been sitting in the Sculpture Garden in late afternoons and seeing the sun filter through the purple blooms of jacaranda, surely one of the most beautiful sensory treats possible.

Thanks to Paul's foresight, Sun Valley now satisfied her desire for changing seasons. With their modest Santa Monica home long since paid for, she could take her time deciding what she wanted to do with the rest of her life.

She remembered reading Caitlin Thomas' book, written after the death of her famous poet husband, Dylan Thomas. Entitled *Leftover Life to Kill*, it was about as passionate a cry of grief as any she'd ever read. She'd only been twenty-five when she read it, and had been struck by a view of life so alien from hers. She couldn't imagine wanting to die if a partner did, no matter how much she loved him. She'd always been repelled by accounts of the Indian tradition of suttee. She could not imagine hurling herself on a burning pyre after the death of a husband. How smug she'd been, disdaining the anguish of widows.

Now she knew. Now she knew. Still, she refused to waste any of her precious time on this earth, so in her practical way, she was picking up the pieces and going ahead. Always too ready to cry at the slightest hint of sentiment, she'd not yet cried the way she thought she would.

She thought she had been so ready for Paul's death, for a final sense of peace after the years of hope and disillusion, the finding and conquering of tumors, only to find and conquer new ones, the experimental procedures, the suspension of disbelief that any of the radical treatments he underwent would work. In the end they hadn't, and, exhausted, Paul had died at home.

When she leaned over his bed to say her last "goodbye," she expected a flood of tears. They didn't come. Instead she felt a crushing sense of grief and shame. Where were the tears? She knew the time would come when she would wrestle with her devastating loss, with the cruel acceptance that he would never sleep next to her again. And yet, she felt a kind of relief. The next day she caught herself making an appointment to have a root canal procedure she'd been postponing for years. Why, in the midst of funeral arrangements, had she made this appointment? Some shrink could have a field day with her, she was sure.

*   *   *   *

Juliet put the coffee cup in the dishwasher, closed the door, took out a box of large green trash bags from under the sink, and went downstairs to their bedroom. She'd been through the sorting out of Paul's things in Santa Monica: there she had her daughters and good friends to help, laughing when they finally disposed of the torn T-shirts he so loved because of their softness. Now she opened Paul's closet and noted the dusky smell, Paul's smell. He'd quit smoking over ten years ago but there was still something woodsy or smoky in the fabric of his clothes. It was pure male, she thought, as she carried an armful of jackets, parkas, and ski pants to the bed. They were a tad out of date, but she was sure someone would be happy to wear them this winter. She planned to donate them to The Gold Mine, the local thrift shop run by the Community Library.

She carefully folded them in the bags, and then opened his chest of drawers. encountering the kind of chaos Paul's drawers always showed. Even as he got weaker and she suggested she put away his things, he insisted on washing and folding his own clothes. And here they were, in scrunched up bunches, unmatched socks lacking mates probably thrown in other drawers. When they were first married, she had tried to organize his clothes for him, bought neat little wooden drawer dividers and carefully placed his underwear and socks in military order. Her efforts lasted about six months, until, after a heated argument over how he was violating her sense of order by allowing the Jockey shorts to commingle with the sweat socks, leaving tops on loosely when he put jars back in the refrigerator, and, worst of all, not putting the new roll of toilet paper on when he finished with the existing one, she had a temper tantrum unlike any she had indulged in since childhood.

"O.K., Paul. You like things messy, well see how you like this!" she had said as she stormed into the kitchen. There she grabbed one of her hand-me-down iron skillets, one lovingly coated with a patina from years of proper seasoning, allowing the grease to settle into the metal, leaving a grimy residue. She brought it back into their bedroom, opened one of the sloppy drawers, and threw it in with the clean socks.

"There!" she yelled, turning away from what she thought would be his rage. Instead, he laughed, and that made her even angrier, but she couldn't stifle the accompanying giggles that rose unbidden from somewhere deep inside her where she still had a sense of humor. The incident became one of those family stories they told their daughters in illustration of the silly people that they had once been.

After that, Juliet gave up trying to make him be as neat as she thought a man should be. Her lingerie could still be placed in scented cubbyholes, her bikinis organized according to style and brevity, and, yes, she got used to being the one always to change the toilet paper. At least that way, it was placed so one pulled the sheets from over the roll instead of from under, which drove her crazy.

＊　　　＊　　　＊　　　＊

She had had the great good fortune to marry a man with a sense of humor. Looking back on their years together, she understood that that was what had kept them together when others were parting.

She didn't articulate this until many years after their marriage. On the road one time they had had to pull over off Highway 101 near Salinas because they both were laughing so hard at a Dave Barry column she was reading him from the Sunday paper. Amidst howls at the humor of Barry's encounter with a horse, Juliet leaned over to her husband, wiped the bit of spittle he'd added to his pathetic attempt at a beard, and said, "Oh my God! I just now understand why I really love you. It's because we laugh together so well!"

When she'd met Paul at UCLA on a Friday afternoon TGIF Bridge game, she had no idea that the guy with the easy laughter would become her husband. She never considered that what would last between them was due to his ability to see the oddity of behavior in life as funny.

So many of her friends had married as she did, without knowing their new mates very well. They thought that a man who was a good dancer, or handsome, or able to engage in brilliant academic repartee was the person of their dreams. Only later did her sisters find out that the qualities they'd sought in a mate met at college might not be the qualities that would provide the best husband. In her case, she was surprised to learn that the more she found out about Paul, the more she loved him.

Her generation expected to get an MRS degree at the same time they were to prepare for nursing or teaching or some other acceptable female vocation. And in her era, the MRS came without benefit of intimacy. They were rather naïve, much as their mothers had been, the only difference being that society now gave them a way out of an unhappy marriage.

The image of Paul, a broad grin on his uneven features, appeared as if he'd just walked in the room. Juliet sat down on the king-sized bed and closed her eyes for a minute.

.And there he was, 21 again, picking up his beer from the bridge table and slipping onto the piano bench while he waited out his turn at being dummy. She was seated at the next table of four, partnered with her friend Dorothy, who was a bridge whiz. At the moment, Dorothy was playing out a three-no-trump hand with ferocious intensity, so Juliet had a moment to look at the young man who had just started playing "Frankie and Johnnie." He rolled his eyes and sang with vigor, though no one joined him. She wanted to.

Later, when her partner became irked that Juliet had under-bid a small slam, she took a break. Paul was through with his game and sitting on the worn leather sofa, slowly sipping another beer. Juliet sat down on the far end of the sofa, picked up a torn copy of *Playboy* and thumbed through it. She tried not to look at the centerfold.

"Juliet? Hey, Juliet," Paul said, putting his beer on the coffee table.

"How do you know my name?"

"Not very hard to figure out, especially when your friend keeps saying, 'Jeez, Juliet'."

She smiled. "I guess today's not a very good bridge day for me. How did you do?"

"O.K. But I'd rather spend time getting to know you."

His directness unnerved her. "Gosh, sure … I'm such a card shark!" Where, she thought, was her sense of wit and intelligence? *I sound like a real jerk.*

He just stared at her. She folded the magazine, put it back on the coffee table and smoothed her skirt. He still stared at her. Finally she returned his gaze, a bit obliquely.

"So, um, where did you learn to play the piano like that?"

"Like what?"

"Oh, you know. So free and bubbly."

He moved closer to her. "Well, you see, when my dad was assigned to the Foreign Service in Algiers, he used to take me to the Casbah with him, And I got to know Hoagy Carmichael. I'll never forget his advice to me: 'Son,' he said, 'always keep your wrists loose'."

"Sure, and I'm Lauren Bacall. No, really." She looked closer at him, his smile slightly crooked, his nose a bit too large, heavy eyebrows, a crew cut. Not her type of looks. But a nice face, little laugh lines already at the corners of his eyes.

To her surprise, he stood up and walked to the piano, sat down and then, with a flick of his head, motioned her over. He started playing "Sweet Sue," the song she and her sorority sisters had sung at Spring Sing.

"Ah yes, Lauren," he said, "and I learned many other tricks in the Casbah, like how to learn a lot about someone before you even meet her ... especially if you want to meet her."

And that was it. Two months later they were pinned, then endured an anxious year while he served in the Army Reserve in Virginia. By the time they were married, they had really only spent a few weeks together, most of it intense with partings and reunions. So when they married, just two months short of the two years they had been together, they didn't know each other very well at all.

So, yes, she'd been lucky that that lanky, off-center, almost homely piano player had turned out to be such a good man, so much looser than she, so ready to accept her entirely for what she was.

In homage to Paul, she decided to toss all the contents of the bureau in one bag. "Let someone else sort it out," she thought. While pouring out the mess of clothes at the bottom drawer, she picked up a piece of paper stuck to its bottom. It was an old wrapper from a soft drink mix called Louie Lollipop. She felt a sharp stab in her chest. Paul had put it in her mailbox at school her first year of teaching, more than 25 years ago. The sprawling ballpoint handwriting was still legible. "Louie loves you. And so do I, P."

How had he saved this all this time? How come it was all the way up here in Sun Valley in 1998 instead of at home in her memories' box? Oh, Louie, Louie.

CHAPTER 2

▼

The wind slapped Juliet's face and she wrapped her sweatshirt closer to her thin frame.

"So you got it all done, then," said Barbara Marks, as the two of them and Spanky, Juliet's golden retriever, walked against the wind on the Malibu shoreline.

"Enough for now. Things are cleared out for the renters, you know, personal stuff crammed into the storage closet. But I did get rid of a lot of junk." Juliet halted, bent over and retrieved a salmon-pink shell. She tucked it in her pocket.

"Good. I just hope you don't overdo it. You've lost some weight."

Juliet had, indeed, shed some pounds recently, and her calico blond hair was streaked with a few more gray hairs.

"I know. I know," Juliet replied. "It's like your divorce diet, remember?"

"Yep! Grief and disappointment will do it every time. It's a sure way to cast off a few ugly pounds along with other ugly things. But still, I'm worried about you."

"Don't worry. I'll be fine." Juliet bent to pick up a twig and tossed it far in front of her. It landed in the water. Spanky ran to retrieve it and returned, slobbery and wet.

"Who are your renters?"

"Sam and Betsy Duncan. From New Hampshire. I don't know them, but they sound great. He's a professor at Dartmouth; she's an artist. Now I'm glad we have a fairly big place. For what I will get in rent for those two weeks, I can take the girls to Mexico."

"How do they feel about this?" Barbara looked at her friend.

"They seem fine with it. Whatever doubts they might have about strangers in the house seem to fade away when they think about Mexico."

Without a verbal agreement, both women turned and headed back towards Barbara's house. They knew the routine by now, had been taking this walk at least once a week for more than twenty-five years, ever since they were young teachers at Santa Monica High School. Juliet had stayed in teaching after their first hectic years, but Barbara had left after two years when she was offered a job as a gofer for a small documentary film production company. Now she was, two marriages and three children later, a producer of award-winning documentaries. Juliet had always envied her friend's courage in leaving the comparatively secure world of teaching for the then-uncharted waters of being a woman in the world of film. Juliet fell into the comfortable rhythm and reverie that a long walk often induced.

As they approached the side gate and Barbara's driveway, and she found her keys in the deep sweatshirt pocket, Juliet studied her friend once again. With shiny black curls and what one gently called a "zoftig" figure, Barbara was a vivacious bundle of energy that still attracted men, even though she was approach-

ing fifty and single. Juliet didn't know how she got the energy
to keep up the mating game. She tucked away a twinge of envy
for her friend, "dating" exciting men, getting to go to film festivals every year, now living on Broad Beach Road with lots of
celebrities for neighbors. She had actually been able to buy one
of the houses they used to admire when they had taken these
walks in their twenties. She felt dull in comparison. Married to
one man in a monogamous relationship, most of her adult years
spent teaching English and raising her daughters and being
fairly conventional. Even now she didn't have the daring of her
friend.

Barbara lingered by Juliet's car window.

"You're sure you don't want to stay for another cup of coffee?"

"No, thanks, Barb. I've got errands,"

"O.K." She still paused at the window as Juliet started the
car. "I'm having some friends over for dinner next Saturday.
Will you save the evening?"

"Sure … just tell me what to bring."

As she pulled out of the driveway, Juliet glanced back at her
friend and realized Barbara was grinning. It hit her. She had
planned a dinner with some stray eligible man in attendance,
the little sneak.

*   *   *   *

Sitting on Barbara's deck as one of those riotous, deep red
sunsets spread before her, Juliet chuckled at the thought of her
duplicitous friend. Even through the many phone calls of the
past six days, while they planned the menu and the tone of the
evening, Barbara still wouldn't confess to inviting a man for her

friend. But here he was. Actually, there were two unattached men among the people included in the evening. One of them had just joined her on the deck, leaning against the weathered railings, bougainvillea framing his handsome shape. She reminded herself that "handsome" had never been her style.

"May I get you a refill of what ever it is you've got there?" His voice was pleasant enough.

"No, thanks. I'm fine." She looked up at him, noting all the visual components of the pretty picture. "I'm Juliet. I apologize for not getting your name when we met inside ... I'm, terrible with names; I hate that quality. I always admire people who remember my name—I think it's really a sign of respect. I had some friends who worked for Robert Kennedy. They used to talk about the Kennedy quality of remembering names, how it made people feel special and honored that he would take the time to learn names. A simple practice, but one that is so magical, I think. Don't you?" She'd gone on about this so. Embarrassed, she glanced at her glass of soda, twisting it in her hand.

"My name's Jim. Jim Milton. And I will remember your name!" He laughed, and turned towards the sunset.

"What do you do, Jim?" God, she felt like she was back in college, asking someone what his major was, but she realized she hadn't practiced chitchat for awhile, at least not with a potential date. Date! She hadn't even thought about dating, and here she was, getting tongue-tied at the attention of the first man since Paul. She was ashamed of herself.

"I'm a writer: screenplays, mainly, though I do have a novel tucked away for constant revision."

"Oh. My husband is ... was ... a writer, a journalist."

"Oh? I didn't realize you were married. Is he hiding in the kitchen?"

"No. He died six months ago. Of cancer. But it's O.K.," Juliet hastened to add, when she saw his cheek twitch. "You couldn't have known."

As if on signal, Barbara emerged to announce dinner, and Juliet excused herself to help in the final serving.

The evening turned out to be a wonderful one ... the mix of people just right. Juliet always felt at home with Barbara, in spite of the luminaries who often found themselves at her table. She actually enjoyed carrying on conversation with the young television actress and her director lover, didn't even feel "less than" because she had "only" been an English teacher, now no longer even working at that. She didn't feel she had to tell anyone there that she had stopped her beloved teaching five years ago when Paul became ill.

*   *   *   *

Two weeks later she met Jim at the Beverly Wilshire for a drink. He had called her several times, and she had finally agreed to meet him on this neutral ground. After about an hour of polite, slightly charged conversation, he asked her out for dinner later in the week. She agreed, amidst a wash of guilt and denial.

Now she sat across from him at Locanda Veneta at, he insisted, one of the "good" tables. He was telling her about the complicated deals involved with his latest screenplay, a futuristic epic about life in a very organized and sterile society.

"So finally, Sima escapes from her home, but it takes intensive planning. I mean, she's not just allowed to go to the market or anything. She's supposed to remain behind her four walls and breed. When she gets out there, though, she realizes she has nowhere to go, no one to hide with, so she comes back."

"Sounds like *Brave New World*, the *Stepford Wives* and *The Handmaiden's Tale* all mixed together," she mused, not sensing the rigidity of his back.

"Well it isn't. It's my original idea."

"Oh, sure, I know. I'm sorry. It's the old English teacher syndrome, I guess. Can't help but find connections in works of literature. I didn't mean anything derogatory."

"I'm sure you didn't," Jim muttered, as he looked over her shoulder at a couple coming in the room. "Oh, there's Jodi and her agent. Hi, Jodi."

While Jim turned his attention to the others, rising and going over to the table at which the couple had been seated, Julie rested back on her chair. *I just can't do this,* she thought. *I hate this dating stuff; I don't know what to say. I either say too much or the wrong thing.* She was glad when he spent most of the remainder of the evening waving at other diners and smiling at latecomers. She couldn't wait to get home, take a hot bath, cuddle Spanky and open a good book.

So that had been her first foray into the "Brave New World" of dating in the nineties. Well, she wasn't interested. Manzanillo, Mexico, with her daughters, safe and warm, beckoned.

CHAPTER 3

▼

The phone was ringing. She rushed in from the garage through the back door of the clapboard bungalow on 20th Street, barely missing a fall from catching the edge of the area rug. Why did she still hurry to get a phone? She knew the caller would leave a message on her phone machine, but old habits died hard, and years of feeling the need to respond to the urgent sound of a telephone ring still compelled her to interrupt whatever she was doing at its beck and call.

"Hello? Hello?" she panted into the wall phone near the sink.

"Juliet? This is Oliver Simms. Is this a bad time?"

"No, no. Just give me a second, O.K.? I just came in from the market, and I need to shake out the rain. What's it like there?" Julia asked, as she juggled the phone while removing a rain-soaked cardigan.

"No sign of snow yet, but it's pretty gloomy. Typical early November weather for Sun Valley. Had you planned on Thanksgiving up here?"

Juliet used the few moments of Oliver's conversation to ease groceries out of the shopping bags.

"I don't think so. My daughters are planning to be here that weekend. Besides, I want to save my pennies for Mexico." She elbowed open the refrigerator to her left and hefted a pork tenderloin into the meat drawer.

"O.K. I'm glad I called, then. Seems there is a problem with the December rental. At least we have the deposit ... I just sent it to you, as a matter of fact."

Cradling the phone on her shoulder, Juliet reached to the right and opened the trash compactor, tossing in a few leftover tidbits from the sink. Then she wiped down the sink with paper towels.

"What kind of problem?"

"The Duncans can't come. Seems Mrs. Duncan is ill, and they are too involved with doctors and tests right now to think of a vacation in December. Sam Duncan told me to tell you not to worry about returning the deposit. It's yours, certainly. He's a really nice man, Juliet. I'm sure he's telling the truth. Do you want me to find another rental?"

"Let me think about it, Oliver. I'm just so sorry to hear about their troubles. I was sort of set on them as prospects for my first rental. I'm not sure about letting anyone else in there now. I'll call you back in a couple of days, O.K?"

"Sure. I'm so sorry. I'm sure we can do the job for you, though. Just let me know."

After Oliver Simms hung up, Juliet let in Spanky and wiped his muddy paws with a ragged towel she had ready on a hook by the back door. Then she warmed her leftover latte in the microwave and sat at her kitchen table. She had really liked the idea of that family. Sam Duncan, Dr. Sam Duncan, and his wife Betsy, had impeccable credentials. They had gone through all the correct channels with the real-estate company, but they also had sent her a very gracious personal letter, and she had been impressed. They had two grown sons, one married and living in Maine and one still unattached, practicing medicine at Dartmouth College hospital. They had planned a family skiing trip for the full two weeks of Christmas. They must be disappointed. She hoped Mrs. Duncan's illness wasn't serious. Certainly she wouldn't keep the deposit. She was sure they'd need any extra cash for medical bills, especially if it were serious. She would write them a little note in addition to returning their deposit.

Spanky settled in by her feet.

The phone rang again. This time she allowed herself the luxury of monitoring the call. She heard the honeyed male voice, "Juliet? If you're there, please answer. It's Jim."

It had been a week since their "date." She hadn't expected to hear from him again. Juliet let the phone call hang on the line until Jim hung up. She was surprised he was still interested.

Spanky leaned his jaw over her right foot. She recalled Barbara's observation that the litmus test of a relationship was whether she'd rather be with her dogs for an evening at home than out with whomever her current lover was. Juliet had laughed. Now she knew what that meant.

She took out a package of lamb chops from the freezer to thaw, went to her small slant-top desk and began a note to the Duncans.

*   *   *   *

"What other things have you done beside teach?" John Slade, Director of marketing for the new Lion Cable TV Company, said as he shuffled through her resume.

"I've written a lot, just not published, and I've been active in the community," Juliet replied. "But if you think teaching is ALL I've done, let me remind you that I created stimulating lessons for over 150 adolescents. That requires the kind of skills which I'm sure are good for many other occupations." Said with a false cheeriness, the words might as well have had exclamation points after them.

"I mean professional skills, Mrs. Barnes."

"So do I. Creativity, imagination, organization, dealing with a variety of people every day, those are just some of the things needed to be a good teacher."

"Yes. Well, thank you for your time. We'll let you know if anything develops," Slade said, rising from his chair and extending a hand to Juliet."

As she left the high-rise offices on Wilshire Boulevard, Juliet thought that all the companies she'd applied to must have taken lessons together in how to politely turn down someone who had been "just" a teacher. The same lowering of the lids, the same courteous but cool demeanor, the same "what ELSE can you do?"

Luckily she didn't have to get a job right away. She was trying to do something other than teach, for her own growth and invigoration, even though she missed the classroom.

As she left the underground parking structure into the bright sunlight of Brentwood, Juliet headed her small car west towards home and a long conversation with Barbara. Then she'd enjoy a hot bath and preparations for her evening with an old friend of hers and Paul's.

Andrew Simpson had surprised her with a phone call the day after Thanksgiving. Juliet had been polishing her mother's sterling and putting it back into the silver drawer when the phone rang. Waiting to hear who was on the line, she had not at first recognized the deep voice.

"Juliet? This is Andrew—Andrew Simpson. I've been meaning to check up on you since the funeral. I'm in town for a few days and thought perhaps we could get together. Catch up, you know? Please call me at my hotel. I'm at the Century Plaza.... room 325. I look forward to hearing from you."

An hour later Juliet returned his call. Andrew and Paul had been friends in college where Andrew was known for his quiet and studious manner. He'd married a girl he met from Ohio during her summer school session at UCLA, and they'd settled in Columbus. Over the years they'd kept in touch, and every time Ohio State played in the Rose Bowl, the Simpsons had come out to California, and they invariably had dinner together.

"Andrew? Hi, it's Juliet. How nice to hear from you. What brings you out here?"

"Oh, just some personal matters. Say, why don't you come over to my hotel and we'll have a drink, then go somewhere good for dinner? How does that sound?"

"Sounds great, Andrew. Where's Linda?"

"I'll tell you all about it when we meet. Just call up to my room about 7:00. I should be through with my meeting by then."

"Sure, see you later."

Now, as the parking attendant handed her a ticket, and Juliet walked up the stairs of the sweeping, curved hotel, she experienced some qualms. Why had she agreed to come to his hotel? Why didn't she just meet him at a restaurant? Where was Linda? Oh, heck! Who did she think she was? Some femme fatale? Nothing could go wrong.

Stifling the urge to think of a last-minute excuse to cancel the date, Julie went to one of the lobby in-house phones and dialed room 325.

"Andrew Simpson here."

"Hi, Andrew. It's Juliet. I'm here." *Duh*, she thought, *of course I'm here or I wouldn't be calling.* Her inner editor was active, as usual.

"Hi, Juliet. Can you come on up? Something just waylaid me here and I'm not ready."

What was the sense she was having that sent up her antennae? Why did she feel queasy? After all, they had been friends for a long time. "Sure. I'll be up shortly."

Andrew opened the door a few minutes later, a towel wrapped around his hips. "So sorry, Juliet. Come on in. He leaned toward her and placed a brotherly, almost-air-kiss, on her cheek. "I took the liberty of ordering us some drinks. Please sit down while I finish dressing. There's a pitcher of martinis on the coffee table. I thought I remembered you liked Stolichnaya vodka, so that's what's there."

Feeling trapped, Juliet sat down on the small hotel sofa and poured herself a drink while Andrew babbled on behind her as he dressed.

Soon enough, he emerged from the closet and came over to the sofa. He sat down next to her and poured himself a drink.

"I made reservations at Chez Michel. I hope that meets with your approval. Well, here's to old times, my friend." He raised his glass in toast and looked her in the eyes.

"Here's to old times, yes," said Juliet, avoiding his stare. "Speaking of which, it seems strange to see you without Linda at your side."

"And you without Paul. Look, Juliet, I feel funny talking about this, but Linda and I are separated." He stood up and walked to the window, looking out at the sunset while he continued. "We had been apart in many ways for a long time. I don't know why, but once the kids went away to college, there didn't seem to be anything left to talk about. We both started pursuing other interests, I guess. Hers involved a personal trainer she hired to come to the house."

He returned to the sofa, placing himself closer to her than he'd been before. "Being a cuckold is very uncomfortable."

He didn't look at her this time but drew rings on the table in the moisture from her drink. He fixed her another.

Juliet didn't know what to say except "I'm sorry. Are you still living together?"

"Yes, but in name only. One of the reasons I'm out here is to tend to some investments I've made over the years in California real estate. We're going to have a settlement conference soon." Now he moved even closer, reached over to hold her chin gently and said, "But the important thing is how YOU are feeling. Paul's death must have been horrible."

Wavering between gratitude that she could remind herself that this was an old and dear friend whose attentions surely were brotherly and the growing suspicion that they were not, Juliet turned her head away from him so that he had to take his hand off her chin. He put it on her shoulder.

"Yes, it was. Five years take their toll on everyone." Now she was angry that she wasn't asserting herself or getting up from the sofa.

"Juliet, please look at me."

She turned her head back toward Andrew, trying to read what was in his eyes.

"I have to say this," Andrew said, as he poured more Stoli into her glass. "After we talked at the funeral, I had this over-whelming need to take you in my arms, especially when you clung to my arm, after the way you held on to me. I wanted to make up for all the years you'd suffered.

"You didn't know it, but I had already found out about Linda's affair. I knew that the timing was wrong then, but I've given it some thought and now I have to let you know that I've always loved you. Oh, I loved Linda, sure, but there was an ideal woman of my dreams who never left them. Now that Paul is gone, I'd like you to consider that I am free and willing to help you through this time of readjustment. I know you are attracted to me, too."

Juliet stared at him. Was this the Andrew she and Paul had counted as a friend—the shy person she thought she knew? How dare he misread her friendship, assume such things. Here she was, in his hotel room, listening to this shocking news with what must have seemed like aplomb. Her heart was beating rap-idly, but not from love or even lust. From rage.

She recognized it as an alien emotion. She hadn't had the luxury of rage for a long time. She hadn't felt she could scream at the doctors who used long Latin terms to avoid telling her that Paul was dying. She couldn't pull out the cords of the machines that were causing him such pain. She couldn't even yell at God because every time she started to she had to remind herself of how Paul was clinging to a small thread of hope, and in some superstitious way she was afraid she might break it with her blasphemy. No, she hadn't expressed any anger for a long time. Well, here it rose, like vomit in her throat.

Andrew waited for her response and put his arm behind her, touching her shoulder.

Juliet stood up, feeling slightly dizzy. She found herself not saying what she felt. Instead, in the good-mannered way she had been trained to talk to men, she muttered, "Andrew, this was a mistake. I'm just not ready for anything. I can't even absorb your separation from Linda, much less the emotions you have told me you have for me. I'm sorry, I think you have misread me. I think I'd better go now." She grabbed her coat and purse from the edge of the sofa and headed towards the door. To her consternation, Andrew had already moved to block the door.

"Please, Juliet. Don't go. I know I shouldn't have spilled all this out so quickly. I couldn't help myself. When I saw you, all I wanted to do was touch you and then let you know what was in my heart."

"Please let me go," she said, trying to move his elbow.

"Not yet. Please hear me out." He wouldn't move, was intractable.

"No?" Now tears she hated flowed. Every time she'd ever been angry this was her reaction. The act of crying, of course, weakened whatever authority she may have had in any argument, but she couldn't help it. Now she was angry with herself as well as with Andrew.

"I'm leaving, Andrew. I can't believe this whole episode. Please be a gentleman and let me out." She turned her face up to his and locked his eyes with hers. She couldn't waver.

"O.K, Juliet. Have it your way." His mild countenance changed suddenly, to Juliet's surprise, as he moved away from the door. "Stupid prick-teaser. You just made a big mistake!"

Juliet fled the room, ran to the elevator and kept herself composed until she had tipped the parking attendant. Then, as she drove out of the curved driveway towards Pico Boulevard and home, she had to pull over the car. She sobbed into the steering wheel, the ugly scene and what she should have done replaying in her mind. She knew now she shouldn't have gone up to his room. But she had been naïve, thought they were merely friends, took him at his word. When he had drinks ready she should have seen it as a warning sign. When he sat too close to her she should have left then. All the moments replayed themselves over and over, sickening her, making her feel tawdry and tainted and as though she had asked for his move at seduction. She felt like a college girl caught in a fraternity room party with someone she didn't like: she felt nineteen and vulnerable. But as she looked into her rear-view mirror she knew she was just a middle-aged woman, attractiveness waning, who had succumbed to flattery and a man's machinations. She <u>was</u> stupid. She couldn't wait to get home to her own bed. It would be awhile before she would let herself be so stupid again.

CHAPTER 4

▼

December 21:

Dear Duncans,

I hope this Christmas time finds you and your family at peace
and well rested. I know that Betsy's been ill, so I wanted to add
my wishes for her speedy recovery to the many you must already
have received.

I haven't met any of you but feel somehow connected to you.
Perhaps it is because I pictured your family as being the first to
rent my home in Sun Valley, and you seemed to fit there in my
mind's eye.

At any rate, I just wanted to get off this postcard from hot and
humid Manzanillo to wish you a happy New Year.

We are having a wonderful time ... so good just to be with my
two daughters for a few days of sun.

Juliet Barnes

"Mom, could you get some sun block right there between my
shoulder blades?"

"Sure, Honey." Juliet reached into the string bag and pulled out the super sunblock tube, squeezed some into her palms and reached across the towel to rub the white cream in the flat spot beneath Tasha's bikini straps. She felt the fine skin, noted the sharp bones of her daughter's shoulder blades and recalled how self-conscious she'd been at that age about her own thinness. Now it was in style. Tasha, her 23-year old honey-blond girl, was surely in style. Juliet felt a pang of loss for her younger child, now grown up, a graduate student at Harvard, studying foreign relations, of all things. How could her little bean have matured so, into this lovely woman?

She helped herself to a healthy slap of sunscreen, remembering how she and her mother used to spend weekends in Palm Springs baking like chickens on spits, back when no one thought of skin cancer. Leaning against the wooden backrest, she watched her other daughter, Jen, swimming easily in the blue ocean waters. Jen's skin was naturally olive, not fair like hers. Her dark short hair gleamed in the reflection off the waves. How fit that she had chosen marine biology as a career, her sturdy water-baby, the 11-month old perfectly at home in the Hawaiian waters on her first vacation nearly 26 years ago.

She tried once more to read the same paragraph in the beach book she'd brought on the trip. *"When they found Rosie MacReady's body, the police also found the strangest murder scene they'd ever witnessed."*

She couldn't concentrate, put the book down, rose from the beach towel and walked to the water's edge. She let herself in waist high, then splashed the water over her breasts and face, enjoying the tingling of salt and cool drops. She stifled the urge to swim out to the gentle waves and join Jen. She thought she swam well enough, certainly used to revel in attacking the waves at Sorrento Beach in Santa Monica, riding them in with her body exalted from the struggle to let go and let the wave take her in. But she hadn't been in ocean water for a long time.

Yes, she had been a good swimmer once. On their honeymoon Paul had praised her ability to jump into the ocean with aplomb. They had spent two weeks on the island of Kauai, about a half-mile from Poipu Beach, two weeks of romance and food and rum drinks and Paul ... the Paul she hadn't ever known to this depth. She hadn't been disappointed at all. She'd heard the jokes about women wondering what all the fuss was about. Not in her case. Paul, tall and tan, with his crooked smile, had proven to be as tender and considerate of her as any bride would have wished. Her awkwardness overcome in the process, she had discovered passions she didn't know she had. Paul. She could see him now, the vibrant young man, striding towards her on the beach, lifting her up and taking her into the water. She could see him. *Paul, Paul.*

Pushing the memory aside, she let herself go in a little deeper, at least enough to float on her back on the buoyant waters. Because the waves broke so far out, she felt some confidence in the strength of the water's hold and leaned back into its grace just long enough to dispel the vision of Paul. Restorative, this trip. She swam out a little way, let herself be carried by a very small wave back towards where she had first entered the water, then shook her hair out and went back to the beach towels where Jen was turning herself over to avoid sunburn.

This felt good. The sand under her feet, the clarity of the water, the company of her daughters. Putting on her sunglasses, she opened the book and began, *"When they found Rosie MacReady's body, the police also found the strangest murder scene they'd ever witnessed."*

*   *   *   *

Jen tossed her small shoulder purse on the couch and let her sandals fall to the tiled floor. "God, that was fun. Corny but fun. I couldn't believe it when the mariachi band started singing 'Cielito Lindo.' Remember when you and Dad used to do that hammy version of it for us whenever we'd take a car trip?"

"Yeah, but I couldn't believe that one of the bartenders asked you out. Good thing you had your engagement ring on."

"He was cute, though. Just think. I could have been number 295 in his gringo-conquest list!"

The three moved out to the deck overlooking the gardens of the vacation development. The grounds housed about twenty small casitas built for tourists. Each had its private pool ringed by hydrangeas and birds of paradise. The lushly landscaped gardens were now lit with soft rosy night lamps, reflecting on the trunks of the palm trees, giving a glow to the dark night sky. Juliet sat down by the small pool and let her bare legs dangle in the warm water. It was 1:30 a.m. and still 80 degrees out. Tasha and Jen sat in big wicker chairs to one side of the verandah and stared at the starry, clear night.

"The thing is," Jen continued, "I didn't know how to act. Thank god for my engagement ring. I didn't feel so rude turning him down. He really was so sweet!" She let a moment of quiet pass. "I miss Tom, but I'm glad I'm here. It's just a little different from Sun Valley." She looked up. "Same clear sky, but I've only got this skimpy dress on!"

"Yep, a bit different," Tasha joined in. She turned her head towards the pool where her mother was making small round puddles on the water's surface. It glowed in the dark night like an amethyst. "Mom? Are you O.K.?"

"Sure, honey. Thanks for asking. I really am. I wish, like your sister, that I had the man I love with me, too. But it's O.K. Really. I'm trying very hard to just enjoy the daily pleasures, you know? Your dad is hardly ever out of my thoughts, but he can't be here, and that's that. I'm so lucky to have you both with me."

"Mom, I didn't mean that I didn't want to be here. I do: even without Tom, I'm glad I'm here. It feels good just to be with you and Tasha this Christmas. Please. I hope you didn't take me wrong."

"Of course I didn't. I know what it's like to be in love and want that person wherever you are. And, I guess I'd better appreciate this time with you both, because once you get married, you'll have other commitments.

"Think I'll go on up to bed. Past my bedtime. If you night owls want to stay down here, that's fine." She rose and stretched. "Nite. I'll see you sometime in the morning. I'm probably going to the outdoor market. If you decide to get up early enough, I'd love you to come with me."

She kissed each girl goodnight and walked up the winding stairs to the master bedroom suite. She turned on the fan, dropped her simple loose linen shift on the floor, picked it up and hung it in the open closet, and sat down on the edge of the huge bed, clad only in her cotton underpants. She'd shower tomorrow morning. Right now she wanted to just slip into the cool sheets and think quietly for a few moments. The breeze stirred the sheer curtains and she thought she could make out the sliver of the new moon in the space where they didn't quite close. Sir Patrick Spense's new moon "with the old moon in its arms." She let the peace of the day pull over her as she closed her eyes and took in the sensation of the soft pillow and slightly scratchy sheets next to her body. She turned on her side, realizing she was only occupying the space on the left side of the bed, so used to being on that side through the years of her marriage. Even now she couldn't bring herself to move to the center of the bed, to stretch out her legs as far as she wanted. She reached over to the empty pillow where, for so long, she had seen that head of thick brown hair, put her arm over to it, and allowed some sadness in. Funny, she could recreate the smell of her mother's perfume twenty years after she died, and now she could almost feel the thick hair, the feel of his warm cheek, her hands on his neck and then on the hair of his chest, reassuring and strong somehow. She tried to imagine his smell but couldn't. It was enough to sense his warmth and male quality. She let her hand rest on the empty pillow for a few moments, felt the tears wetting her side of the bed, and turned over.

*   *   *   *

She was a morning person, always had been. She used to correct most of her students' weekly compositions at 4:30 in the morning before everyone else woke up. She found that she could do them in half the time if she was sitting at her kitchen table with a first morning cup of coffee, the quiet resulting from people in deep sleep, and the heavy dark of the night around her. Now she awoke at about 8:00 a.m., luxurious sleeping in for her, showered, dressed and walked the two miles to the mercado.

When she arrived at about 9:00, it was already busy. Vendors called out their goods, women in bright cottons looked cautiously at baskets of produce, and many shoppers stopped to gossip with their neighbors. Juliet felt here something she missed in the relative isolation of life in Los Angeles. She suddenly thought of Sun Valley, which always felt like a small town to her. There, as here, people bumped into each other all the time at the market and at the post office, daily connections.

Sure, she had neighbors and a close circle of friends in L.A. as well, lots of people to talk with, but often she spoke with them only by telephone or by carefully laid plans. Everyone was spread out in the sprawling city. Even her best friend, Barbara, lived 18 miles away. In Mexico one sensed the daily contact of friends and neighbors. She understood enough Spanish from her stint with Mrs. Silva in high school to get the gist of most conversations.

They were talking about food, prices, and the weather. This really isn't that much different, she imagined, from the daily conversation of most people in the world. Sometimes she thought she was overly sentimental about people who led "simpler" lives than she. She fancied herself part of a tribe, sitting on banks with other women washing clothes and experiencing the kind of deep connection of, say, women in quilting bees. She knew that was foolish and probably smug or condescending. She should not assume things about others' lives. She had her life and they had theirs. She certainly didn't envy the poverty that so many of these women experienced, nor would she really choose to make her life more elemental if she were given a choice. Nonetheless, she craved that kind of closeness.

She wandered through the dusty paths, stopping to look at trinkets, brightly colored embroidered blouses, stands of fresh papaya and bananas, smiling and saying, "Gracias, pero no" at each. When she rounded the end of one aisle, she noticed in the distance at the end of the next aisle a short man dart around the corner, as though he were trying to avoid her discovery. The image frightened her for some reason. *Why should I be afraid? It is morning; people are friendly.*

She ascribed her fears to gringo paranoia, and went on, filling her mesh bag with fresh warm tortillas, Mexican cheese, and a few green chiles. They'd have quesadillas for lunch.

*   *   *   *

Walking back, Juliet dismissed her fears. One spring, early in their marriage, she and Paul had taken a trip to Mexico City. They took a couple of days off to visit Taxco and spend the night in the romantic hotel layered on the slopes of the charming city, known for its silver. The memory of Paul arranging a serenade by wandering guitarists was almost too precious to bear. Perhaps her love for Mexico and her people arose from that balmy evening on the terrace. When they boarded a bus for the return trip to Mexico City, they had been flush with their love and hopes for their new life together. Arriving in the city, they were greeted by a deluge of rain, heavy sheets of water that soaked them when they disembarked. Paul looked in vain for a taxi. After a long time a shiny black Mercedes pulled alongside with a thirtyish couple in front. The woman passenger rolled down her window and asked, in clear English, if they needed a ride. Paul looked at Juliet and they both nodded "yes."

When the kind couple dropped them off at the hotel, they asked if Paul and Juliet would like to be their guests at dinner. Again, both happily agreed. Only later, during dinner, did both Paul and Juliet have similar fears. Perhaps this was a set-up. Naïve young American couple succumbs to the oldest ploy in the tourist trade ... while being dined by new "friends," an accomplice gains entry to their room and robs them blind. What a natural con on unsuspecting gringos!

But when they arrived home and checked their room, their relief was tinged with shame, for nothing was gone. They had just met and spent the evening with wonderful and generous people who were genuinely solicitous of a rain-soaked couple visiting their country. Upon returning to California, they began a correspondence with the Mexican family that still continued.

Ever since that incident, Juliet had been careful not to allow some preconceived notion color her acceptance of another culture. That didn't mean she left her wallet around, but she wouldn't do that traveling in her country, either.

The girls were tanning on lounge chairs by the pool when she arrived. Dropping the groceries on the colorful blue and yellow tiles of the kitchen counter, Juliet called to them through the open window.

'Hi, guys. Ready for some quesadillas?"

"Sure. Do I have time for a swim first?"

"Of course. Oh, and, by the way, I mailed some of our cards. If you want any to arrive home before we do, we'd better put them in the mail again tomorrow."

"Thanks, Mom. Think I'll call Tom, though. He's probably home this morning," Jen said, as she arose to go in the cool living room.

Juliet could hear Tasha's smooth cut of the water as she dove into the tepid pool.

Over the steamy fresh quesadillas, Juliet looked at her two daughters. How lucky she felt to have these people as friends ... not just daughters, but friends. She told them all about the market this morning, wishing in the process that they'd awakened early enough to go with her. She knew better. Her kids had a different body time clock than she did. They'd always been night owls. Luckily she and Paul had both been morning people. Maybe that's what held their marriage together. She couldn't have imagined life on a daily basis with someone who could not abide her cheery morning demeanor.

When she mentioned the suspicious man at the end of the aisle, she minimized her fears. "Do you know how stupid I feel even telling you this? He was probably some person who works here at the resort and recognized me. Oh well, he didn't follow me or anything, so I guess that shows how silly I am."

"Mom," Tasha said, clearing the plates from the table, "It's O.K. You need to honor your feelings. He didn't know how you felt, so you didn't insult him, and it's perfectly all right to share your fears with us."

"You're right, Honey." Tasha was aware of all the most current thinking in psychology, and Juliet sensed the phrase "honor your feelings" came from that. But she was right. She was entitled to have even negative feelings. One didn't always have to be calm and put together and holding up for the sake of others. At least here she could relax and let her feelings out.

"Yep. You should have majored in psychology, Tash."

"Well, I just think you ought to trust us, respect us enough to let us know if you're sad or frightened, Mom."

She was lucky.

*   *   *   *

That night, under the slight moon, she and Jen took a walk along the edge of the dark water. Juliet stopped several hundred yards down the beach to smell the tropics, to feel the warm water tickle her toes, to cherish the feel of her daughter's arm entwined in hers. She actually released Jen long enough to twirl around, relishing the giddiness this caused.

"Mom, what on earth are you doing?"

"Oh, just soaking it all in. You know, the feel of Mexico, this time and this place. I love it so!"

"So do I." Jen traced an outline in the sand. "Did you know, Mom, that along some of the beaches in Baja turtles return to mate and deposit their eggs in the exact spot where they were born? Often it is many years after they have left as infants. Sometimes I fancy myself like one of them, wanting always to return to the beach, where I feel at home."

"I think I know what you mean. The ocean is always soothing to me." Juliet could see the outline of the promontory at the end of the cove more distinctly now. "Is it true that turtles cry when they leave the ocean? I've always meant to ask you about that. Seems like an old wives' tale to me."

Jenny turned her face towards her mother, and smiled. "I wish it were true. It's a lovely tale. Actually, they are getting rid of salt. Turtles have glands close to their eyes that produce salty tears all the time. Of course we can't see them when they are in the water, only when they're out, so we think they are crying."

Juliet sighed, "Oh, shoot. I was hoping the story my mother told me was true. Oh, well. I guess we human beings want to make every living creature in our image."

As they turned around and headed back towards the resort, a glimmer from the adobe wall bordering the beach caught her eye. She stopped, took Jen's arm again and stayed still for a moment. Then, she looked carefully again at the wall. There was no glint. *What a ripe imagination I have!*

"Mom, are you O.K.?"

"Sure. Let's keep walking." She tried to tell herself nothing was wrong, but Juliet couldn't shake the sense of dread she felt. A small shiver ran through her in spite of the warm night. She pulled Jen closer to her and, like a girl, started running down the edge of water and sand, wetting the edges of her sheer cotton dress, then turning towards the safety of the casita, aware now of the presence of eyes from behind.

Only when they were within sight of home did Juliet feel the tears with the salt water on her cheeks.

"Mom. What's the matter?"

"Jen, sweetie. I think your old mom's overdone it. Lets get home."

Feeling suspicious, hating the fear, Juliet was careful not to look toward the wall the rest of the way home, but she felt the burn of brown eyes on her even as she and Jen sang "Cielito Lindo" all the way home.

CHAPTER 5

▼

The next morning, when she padded in bare feet down the wrought iron staircase, Juliet was surprised to see Jen curled up on the sofa. She walked quietly over to her daughter, not sure she was awake.

She noticed the puffy eyes first.

"Honey?" she whispered, "What's wrong?"

"Oh, Mom, it's probably nothing. I'm just blue, that's all."

"What about? Wait. Let me make some coffee and meet you outside. It's a beautiful day already. I'll get you a cool cloth, too."

Juliet went to the kitchen and prepared a carafe of strong Mexican coffee, dampened a washcloth, stifled the fluttering in her heart, and went out to the verandah, where Jen had moved to a lounge chair. She placed the rag on her daughter's hot forehead but was careful not to intrude. Jen had always been private in her emotions.

"Thanks, Mom." She poured sweet cream, added grainy raw sugar and took a sip of the warm coffee. Then she rested back on the reclining slope of the chair.

"Do you want to tell me about it, honey? I'm here to listen, you know."

"Oh, I'm sure it's O.K., but I can't seem to get ahold of Tom. I tried him yesterday at lunch and left a message. Thing is, it's a weekend, and he should have been in bed or just getting up. But anyway, I figured maybe he turned off the machine, so I didn't think about it very much the rest of the day. But then I tried him again before dinner and then after we got in from our walk last night. We had a code. If he had gotten my message, he was supposed to change his recording to reflect what time he'd call me back so I could be here to get the call. His message is just the same."

"Well, maybe he's just busy and knows he can't call you at a particular time. Or maybe he went away for the weekend. I'm sure he's as frustrated as you are."

"Maybe. I hope you're right. But the thing is, Mom, he's been a bit distant lately. I felt kinda bad about leaving, but I trust him, and I just thought this might be our last time for a while to be together as a family. What's left of it, anyway. Because it was our first Christmas without dad and stuff, well, I just thought he'd understand. I mean, I think he did."

"Well, then darling, I'm sure he'll be there for you when we go home."

"I keep telling myself that I'm just imagining things. Yesterday when Tash told you to honor your feelings, I almost said something. Because I just think he's growing away from me. I can't put my finger on it, but when he saw me off at the airport I could swear he was relieved. He didn't say anything, but now he's not home when he should be, and ... oh, Mom. I'm scared. He's everything to me."

Juliet sat at the edge of the lounge chair, and put her hand on Jen's small, muscled thigh.

"Just let your feelings be, honey. There's nothing you can do about it right this minute. We're going home in three days, and there will be plenty of time to sort this out. On the one hand, I want you to put this aside so you can have a good time, but on the other I think Tash is right. It's selfish of me to want you girls to be happy all the time. It makes me more comfortable to see you smile, but life isn't always easy and there may be some pain. I need to let you feel that if you have to. So go ahead and cry if you want."

"Oh, mom, I feel like you don't need this worry about me at this time."

"Yes, I do. That's part of being a mother. I don't want you hurt, but if you are, you have to feel free to express it around me."

Jen let the tears roll while Juliet waited for implied permission, then reached out to hold her daughter's small body as close as she could.

*   *   *   *

After two more days without hearing from Tom, Jen could no longer enjoy the beauty of the hot Mexican sun and vivid sea: her brave façade had disappeared, and both Tash and Juliet were concerned.

Packing for the trip home the next day, Juliet sat down on one of the twin beds in the hacienda's guestroom. She watched Jen toss her things in a duffel bag while Tash carefully rolled her T-shirts and shorts into neat piles and orderly form. *The acorn never falls far from the tree,* Juliet thought, a roll of tenderness like a fist in her chest. She wanted to take Jen's pain on, be like the Jesus she'd loved as a child in Sunday school and bear her daughter's burdens, but she knew she couldn't. She couldn't wrap them in cotton and keep them near, safe from harm. But oh, how she wanted to!

"So, O.K., girls. This is our last night here. I know you're glum, Jen, but let's go to Carlos and Pepe's tonight and splurge on big fat fresh shrimp."

Jen crossed over from her side of the room and sat on the edge of the bed across from her mother. "Sure, Mom. Don't worry about me. I'll be fine. I really think Tom will have a good explanation for everything. I just can't believe he'd hurt me this way. Sometimes men just don't think things through about emotional stuff. It's no big deal to them, so they think it's no big deal to us, right?"

"Yeah," said Tash, not looking right at her sister, "I'm sure when you get off the plane, he'll be there, all hang-doggy."

She nodded in agreement, but Juliet's thoughts were rebellious. *What's the matter with that young man? Can't he see how his lack of concern affects Jen? Anyone who is that thickheaded, even if his reasons are valid, isn't the kind of person who deserves Jen. I'd better keep these mutinous thoughts to myself, though. Meddling mothers only make things worse.*

"O.K. then, we'll go to dinner about 8 o'clock and try to relax." Juliet arose and went directly to the big bathroom adjoining her bedroom. She took off her bathing suit, hung it up to dry, and stepped into the shower. She let the water get hotter than usual, even with the thermometer outside at 85 degrees, and soaked, the water pounding her tense neck and back.

*   *   *   *

In spite of the margaritas, the magenta sunset and the succulent, sweet shrimp, Juliet was glad to return to the hacienda that night. Unspoken sadness had permeated the thick air, and she had found herself fighting back tears. She tried to understand that sadness. She knew it was in part a combination of emotional experiences: the underlying sense of Paul's absence, the anxiety about Tom's lack of connection over the past few days, maybe even some inevitable poignancy at the end of a special time for a mother and two daughters, away from the stresses of life in a warm and beautiful place. Saying "goodbye" to a lovely time was always difficult. But Juliet knew there was more. Under all of this was the bleak knowing that life would never be free of pain for her girls. As adults, her daughters would have to grapple with the unavoidable edge of grief that hovers near every life. They would learn, as she had, how to capture the fleeting moments of peace and beauty and keep them close to pull out and examine when one slipped over the edge.

This time together had been one of those sweet moments, but they were headed back to reality.

As they entered the house, Juliet noticed that something was wrong: the furniture was out of place, and the jacket she had hung over the back of the rattan love seat was gone. Had she taken it upstairs when the girls were packing? No. She recalled deliberately putting it on the love seat so she would not miss it in the morning when they left for the airport.

"Tash, Jen," she said now, her throat drying up with each word. "Don't go upstairs just yet."

She took a few tentative steps toward the stairs.

"Why, what's the matter?" Tasha said, drawing closer to her mother.

"Probably nothing. Bear with me. Probably too many margaritas." She tried to be calm, but the waver in her voice betrayed her nervousness. The girls pulled on her arms. Juliet took them firmly and ran back out the door into the dark street.

As they bolted out the door, they heard a crash from the end of the hall upstairs. Someone was definitely there! They ran across the street towards the neighbors' hacienda, and Juliet commanded, "Jen! Use your good Spanish and call the police. I think we may have been robbed."

The police arrived within ten minutes and, after an inspection of the house, led the three women back inside and upstairs. There they found what they feared: In the girls' room drawers were open, the contents of both duffels spilled on the floor. The camera was gone, as were the few pieces of jewelry they brought. In Juliet's room nothing had been touched. The police told her that they were lucky that they had interrupted the burglar and that they had all been together at the time. Who knows what might have happened had one of them come home alone. The theft of a camera and some costume jewelry seemed inconsequential in the face of the physical harm that could have resulted.

After the police left, Juliet made a cup of cocoa for her daughters and they sat together around the table in the kitchen, recounting the evening's events. Fortunately, Juliet had carried their tickets, credit cards, and remaining cash with her when they went out to dinner. They felt a sense of unease, of violation, for sure. However, as the hours wore on and they stayed the rest of the night in the brightly-lit kitchen, playing gin rummy and nibbling on stale tortillas, they accepted that, all in all, it wasn't that bad. A few things were gone, but they were intact. No one had been hurt, at least by the robbery. Other hurts remained in wait.

*   *   *   *

What a relief it was to open the door of the cottage in Santa Monica. Spanky was even there to greet her. Barbara had delivered him earlier, along with a note. Juliet took time to be slobbered over and nearly knocked down by Spanky's wagging tail, then dropped her keys on the table and glanced at the note.

"Hi, kid. Glad you're back. Spanky was a dream. I have news … BIG NEWS. Call when you can, XOXO, Barb."

Juliet hung up her coat, put fresh water in Spanky's dish, and moved her bag to the laundry room for later emptying. She sat at the table, admitted she was tired, and started to thumb through the mail Barb had put on the table for her. The newspapers could wait until later.

While she sorted the Christmas cards into piles for further reading, answering or not answering, the phone rang. She let it go to the message.

"Hello, Juliet? If you're there, please pick up. It's Barb. I can't wait anymore to talk …"

Juliet picked up the receiver, interrupting Barb's voice.

"Hi. I'm here. Just got in a few minutes ago and had planned to call."

"Good. I'm glad you're back. How was Manzanillo?"

"Terrific, awful. It's a long story. I'll tell you later. So what's up?" Juliet leaned against the counter of the sink while she kicked off her shoes and let her toes be warmed by the thick cotton throw rug beneath.

"Everything. You won't believe it, but I've just met THE MAN. He's it, really, the greatest! Can't wait for you to meet him. When can you come over?"

"Wow! Good news! Can't wait to hear all the gory details. Let's get together tomorrow after I've re-grouped. Oh, and thanks for taking such good care of Spanky."

"You're welcome. Are you O.K? You sound a little down."

"Don't worry. I'm fine ... I'll tell you about it tomorrow. Just a little tired: travel, you know." Juliet suddenly realized she was indeed bone tired, looked at the clock and rationalized that it wasn't too early to take a bath, fix a quick supper and go to bed.

"Well, O.K., pal. I'll let you unwind. But Happy New Year anyway. Love you. I'll call tomorrow and we'll figure out where to meet."

Juliet hung up the phone. She had forgotten that it was January 2 already. The New Year's celebration in Mexico seemed weeks gone by. Because of Jen's sadness she hadn't made much of talk about coming events in the New Year. But it was here, with a vengeance.

The phone rang again. Juliet picked it up immediately.

"Barb, I love you, but I'm going to be a hermit the rest of the evening."

"Mom? It's not Barb, it's me, Jen. Tom's gone. His things are gone."

CHAPTER 6

▼

The fog eddied around the pilings of the Santa Monica Pier as a child might cling to its mother's legs. Juliet found herself creating that simile as she waited for Barbara on a splintery old gray bench overlooking the bay. In spite of its seedy, slightly worn atmosphere, the pier had always been one of Juliet's favorite spots. During her first years at Santa Monica High, she and her teaching friends used to celebrate Fridays with drinks at Sinbad's, her daughters spent many hours riding the merry-go-round at the pier's center, and even today children were still attempting to catch shovel-nosed sharks off its end. It had survived storms and earthquakes, the teardowns of amusement booths, tourists making passes at local girls, numerous movie production crews and equipment, and always the difficulty of parking nearby. It still was an authentic place.

Juliet marveled at how warm it was for January. She noticed the vendors in bright short-sleeved T-shirts. The fog would soon lift, and a bright winter sun raise the temperature to about 70 degrees. So many non-Californians thought the only time to visit its beaches was in the summer. Some of the most wonderful days on the beaches of Southern California were to be experienced in December and January. Quiet of tourists, with clean sands stretched out free of umbrellas and coolers, the coast experienced almost balmy days several times during the winter. Whenever that happened, Juliet tried to take advantage of the rare feeling of being alone on a beautiful beach. Whether Sorrento or Zuma, the beach gave her a sense of calm and release.

She rested her head against the worn fence behind the bench and closed her eyes for a moment, savoring the sounds of gulls, the laughter of children nearby, and the luxury of not having to work—yet—on a weekday morning.

"Hi, kiddo. Long night?" Barbara slipped next to Juliet, two warm coffees to go in her hands. She gave one to Juliet.

"Oh, hi. No." Juliet smiled and reached over to give her friend a loose hug. "Just contemplating for a second. Thanks for the coffee."

"So. I want to hear all about your trip. I've got a meeting with a guy from Miramax at 11:00. More about that later. But tell me. What happened."

"Oh, lots," Juliet replied. "But first I want to hear your good news. Who IS this man? You sounded positively smitten last night."

"I can't wait for you to meet him. He's not in the business, thank god! He's just a normie. Not rich, but not poor. He's a sculptor ... really successful, too. Definitely not a starving artist! I met him three weeks ago when we were scouting locations in Venice for our documentary about the whole LA art scene, you know, with the Getty and other things coming. Anyway, he's this really sensuous, big Italian man. Everything you always thought a sculptor might be, but better."

Juliet looked at her friend's bright eyes and smile. She stifled a cynical comment and took a moment to bask in her friend's pleasure.

"Great! I'm happy for you, Barb. What's his name and when can I meet him?"

"This weekend. Come on out to the house. I'm having a few friends in for a Sunday brunch." She grinned at her friend's expression. "No, I won't have any stray males. Please join us. Oh, and his name? You won't believe it, but it's Giovanni." She cast a look at Juliet for her reaction. "Yes, really. Giovanni Milano. Like the cookie." She gave Juliet a wicked glance. "Tasty, too."

Juliet laughed. Her friend <u>was</u> smitten. She'd reserve judgment on this lothario until she met him. She just hoped Barb wasn't going to be hurt once again.

"So? Now I've told you my news. Or, rather, just the tip of the iceberg. No, not iceberg—volcano is better. But I want to know what's got you down. I thought the trip would be restorative."

Juliet filled her in on the ups and downs of the Manzanillo stay, lavishing her description with details of the place's beauty and the delight she had at being able to be there with the girls, then told of the robbery and, finally what seemed to be Tom's betrayal.

"So, I talked with Jen last night after your call. As of about midnight she still didn't know where he'd gone. He didn't leave a note or anything. Apparently he just packed his bags and left. Poor Jen had a new quarter beginning this week and new research assistants arriving. Maybe it's good she can't sit around and think about that jerk."

"God, I thought he was a terrific guy." Barbara fidgeted with her cup. "You know, interested in her work, very supportive, polite to you, very handsome to boot."

"Honestly, Barb, Sometimes I wonder at my ability to judge people, too. I mean, I thought he was perfect for Jen. I hadn't seen her this happy in years." Juliet drained her cup of the vestiges of foam and crumpled it into a tight bundle. "And, of course, she's devastated. Couldn't he even have had the courtesy to leave her a note—something to at least lessen the pain a bit?"

The sun was shining through the mist, highlighting the reds and yellows of the peeling paint on the sign "Fortunes Told." A booth across the way opened for business; its proprietor, a wizened bald man, threw up the rollaway panel and tied bright balloons to a latch.

"Yeah, it's really hard not knowing." Barb tossed her cup into a wire garbage can, unbuttoned her coat, and resumed. "I've got to go, but I want to hear from you later. I'm really concerned. Is there anything I can do?"

"No. Thanks anyway. I can't even think of anything I can do except be there for her. Sounds like such a cliché! Be there! Hah! She's too old for Mommy to drive up to Santa Cruz and hold her. She's got to learn to get through this. And short of castrating the jerk, there is no way I can pay him back for hurting her so."

Both women arose. Juliet put her arm through Barbara's, still holding the crumpled cup. As they left the asphalt of the pier and stepped on to the clean sidewalk of Ocean Avenue, Juliet searched for a trash can. She spotted one on the opposite corner, then saw a homeless woman leaning against the brick wall behind it. The sign she held said, "Will work for food. Please help." As she came closer to the elderly woman, bundled in rags and newspaper scraps, she tried to avoid her eyes but couldn't. Throwing the cup in the receptacle, she thought she recognized in those blood-shot, hooded eyes the experience of someone she knew. She forced herself to walk by the woman, steeling her heart against the temptation to take her home.

"There but for the grace of God," she muttered, more to herself than to Barb, and the two women walked back to the mall parking lot.

*   *   *   *

Later, Juliet returned to her bungalow. The answering machine's red light was blinking with three messages, one from Jen, another from Tasha, and a third from Ned Walter, Editor-in-Chief of *The Clarion*, the Santa Monica paper that helped launch Paul's career. She listened to all three messages, then replayed Tasha's.

"Hi, Mom. It's Tash. I've heard something about Tom. Call me before you talk to Jen today, if possible. Love you!"

Looking at her HOVIS Bread clock above the bowl of oranges, Juliet noted the hour. The hands were on the "S", 2:00 here or 4:00 in Sommerville, Massachusetts, probably a good time to catch Tasha in her small flat. She often spent the late afternoons home, as her schedule was loaded with morning classes.

She dialed the number. On the second ring, Tasha answered.

"Hi, Honey, Mom. What's up?"

"Oh, Mom. I don't know what to do. One of Jen's friends … you remember Molly? Her roommate from her freshman year in the dorm?"

"Sure. Go on." Juliet poured from some Calistoga on the counter by the sink and sipped.

"Well, she's been going out with one of Tom's friends. He told her she shouldn't tell Jen, but he knows what happened."

"So ... go on. Tell me everything. What do you know?" Juliet shifted her weight and edged off her shoes. Spanky heard the clomp and padded into the room, leaning against her legs.

"Yep. I don't know what to do. Apparently he's living in Monterey with a new girlfriend. She was Jen's research assistant last summer, then left school to get a job at the aquarium."

"Oh, for Pete's sake! Why didn't he at least have the guts to say anything to Jen?"

"I asked Molly that very question. She says everyone's really disappointed in him, but he really didn't tell anyone about it at all." Tasha cleared her throat. "What should I do, Mom? I really think I have to tell her what I know, but I hate to be the one to pull the rug out from under her. And yet, if she hears this from someone else and finds out I knew and didn't tell her, then I know she'll be mad at me!"

"Honestly!" Juliet said, now scribbling concentric circles on the edge of the Eddie Bauer catalog, "This sounds like some junior high intrigue. Maybe I should call her."

There was a pause. Then, "No, Mom. I'll call her. At least she'll feel she can let down, let out her true feelings with me. I'll call her in a couple of hours."

"O.K., Honey. Just let me know what's up. I'll wait for your call before I talk with her."

"Thanks, Mom. Love you—I'll check in with you later."

"Bye, Sweetie." Juliet hung up the phone and walked toward her bedroom.

When she pushed open the heavy paneled door, she sensed the calm of the room quieting her thundering heart. She crossed over the yellow and white hand-loomed Greek rug to the small stereo player on the table next to the bookcase. She inserted a CD of Rubinstein playing Chopin polonaises, and, as the clear notes filled the room, she sat down in one of two matching wing chairs. She and Paul had thought it would be fun to sit by the small corner fireplace together and yet apart enough for good reading, so they bought these two matching pieces and then purchased one big ottoman to share when they read in the evenings. Over the years they had spent many hours reading this way. Juliet turned on the floor lamp and sat down in the worn comfort of "her" chair, the one on the right.

Instead of a book, she picked up a piece of fabric from a large wicker basket at the lamp's base. Scraps of calico and dimity were pinned with needles and thread of varying colors to the 12" x 12" square of muslin, ready for sewing. She felt a semblance of peace as she pulled a piece of bright red thread through the fabric while she appliqued a small representation of an apron on the imaginary kitchen scene she had designed. This was the seventh square she had worked for her "life quilt." It was especially satisfying to be using a piece of fabric for the apron that was actually part of the border of one she had worn when the girls were tiny. The basket on the floor was filled with similar mementos of her life: collars from baby clothes, bits of Oxford cloth from Paul's shirts, and remnants of sheets and upholstery that would always represent important moments. How many times in her life had the simple act of sewing given her time to put her problems in perspective!

She finished the edge of the tiny apron, smiling at the image she had created. That little figure almost looked like her mother, gone now for 30 years. Her girls had never known their grandmother, but she nearly felt her presence here, with the recreation of this domestic scene. What would her mother advise her to do about the pain Jen was experiencing? She could almost hear her say that the only thing she could do was be a listener and a source of strength. Again, women together would find their ways in each generation to absorb the blows life would give them. She had survived her mother's early death, as she knew Jen would survive this hurt. But she still wished it hadn't happened.

Now Juliet decided to add a bouquet of daisies to the counter of the tiny fabric kitchen, and threaded jonquil yellow thread into a needle. As she made French knots for the flowers' centers, she relaxed into the beauty they reflected. If only she could feel as sunny as those blossoms!

*   *   *   *

At 8:45 that night the phone rang and Juliet, beginning to nod off to sleep, jumped at the sound. She put aside the open copy of *Angela's Ashes* from her lap, and answered.

"Hi, Mom? I just finished talking to Jen." Tasha's voice was hurried. "Call her right away. She's waiting to hear from you."

"O.K. But quickly. How did it go?"

"Not well. She's really broken up. But I think she'd already started putting the pieces together. Call me later. X-O-X-O. Bye."

Juliet sipped water from the glass she kept by her bed, and dialed the Santa Cruz number.

"Hello?" Jen's voice sounded hoarse.

"Jen. It's Mom."

"Oh, Mom. I can't stand it!" She paused, a rasping sob in her voice. "I'm sorry. I'm just so sad!"

"Stop apologizing. Just go ahead and cry, Honey. Whatever you need." Juliet waited, maybe 30 seconds, before Jen replied.

"Mom. I can't believe it! How could he be such a jerk, such a coward! And to think he left me for that phony little anorexic Tiffany. That makes it even worse." She spoke between sobs and blowing her nose.

"Oh, Honey. I don't have any answers. The obvious one is the one I don't think you want to hear, but I'll say it anyway." She waited for a sound. "If he could do this now, think what might have happened if you married him. The old platitude says it: Better now than later!"

"I know, I know, Mom. I know all that. But still it hurts so much. You know what I mean? It's physical, even, like a bad cramp in my diaphragm. I can't stop picturing him with that … Barbie doll." A few seconds passed. "Mom? Can I drive down this weekend? Please? I'll get someone to cover for me on Friday. I just want to come home for a few days."

"Sure, Honey. Of course. Just drive carefully. When do you think you'll get here?"

"Probably Thursday early evening. I have a morning class to teach, but then I'll leave around noon."

"Fine. I have a job interview at 4:30. I'll head right home after, and we can have some dinner here. Just don't drive too fast, O.K?"

'O.K. And thanks, Mom. I love you."

"Love you too, baby. See you Thursday."

Juliet arose, picked up the dish with the remnants of her chicken pot pie from the table between the wing chairs, and walked to the kitchen. Then, as she was putting cups and plates in the dishwasher, her eyes caught a dust ball under the break-fast nook table. In spite of herself, she went to the cleaning closet, pulled out mops and sponges, and scrubbed her kitchen floor until it gleamed.

*   *   *   *

Broad Beach had never seemed as pristine, Juliet thought, as she put her plate of eggs Benedict and croissants next to Jen's. What a glorious day! She hoped by now Jen was feeling a little better. Perhaps this calorie-laden meal and some new faces would help.

Biting into the flaky croissant, Julia understood why Barbara was a few pounds overweight. She didn't stint on her appe-tites—never had. Every time the two of them went out, Barb ordered the gooiest item on the menu and never apologized for it, while Juliet looked always for the most healthy entrée, and, oddly enough, the least expensive. Well, today she'd damn the torpedoes and share her friend's lusty appetite. At least as far as food. Having just met Giovanni, she could well imagine how he helped Barb with her other appetites.

Giovanni Milano was a thunderous man. He was big enough to dwarf Barbara, with a deep baritone voice. Barbara said he couldn't sing a note, but Juliet kept expecting him to burst forth in something from *La Boheme* or *Tosca*. Indeed, he was the stereotypically attractive and boisterous Italian man she had occasionally fantasized about in spite of her full and sensuous life with Paul. Here she was doing it again by thinking of such things now.

That very round voice boomed over the sound of the waves as Giovanni approached the round patio table and pulled up a chair next to Jen.

"Cara mia," he said to her, "Barbara tells me you have been having a rough time. Men can be cads, but you are too pretty to waste one minute thinking sad thoughts." He heaped boysenberry jam on his plate and slathered it on his croissant.

Juliet looked at her daughter, saw the tears rush to fill her lids, noted how she stifled them as she replied, "Thanks, Giovanni. But it's not that easy."

"I know, I know. Forgive this silly man from interfering, but I can't help it. You are such a beautiful flower."

"Now, Giovanni. Come on!" Jen replied. Juliet was surprised to see a slight blush to her daughter's cheeks, and perhaps the ghost of a smile.

Well, the old roue! Thought Juliet. *I can't believe she's falling for his baloney. Of course, she is beautiful.*

"No, darling! I won't stop. Life is too wonderful to bother mooning over someone who doesn't appreciate such a work of art."

Juliet let their conversation drift away from her for awhile, just glad to see Jen amused, if even for a moment. She thought of her friend Barb, sitting on the bench on the other side of the deck. She was what one might term "radiant." Wearing a vivid purple tunic-length sheer linen shirt and soft matching pants, big dangly earrings and a rainbow of bracelets she'd brought back from Africa, her friend embodied the happiness of someone in love. She had cut her black hair so it just fluffed around her face, framing her vibrant features and huge eyes.

And, even though he might be a bit overblown, Giovanni seemed mutually in love with Barbara. The more she learned about him, the more she had to agree that he was a suitable match for her friend. Now she heard him push back the chair and saw him go over to Barbara. He folded himself around her and gave her a huge kiss on the cheek.

What Juliet felt at his show of affection surprised her. The sudden knot in her stomach and rush of heat was a sign of envy. She envied her friend. She was jealous, felt dowdy and ordinary in the glow of such vivacity.

"Mom? What's wrong?" She heard Jen say.

"Oh, nothing, Honey. Too much coffee, probably." But she felt a rush of shame. How could she deny her darling friend anything? Barbara, who had nursed her through the hours after Paul's death, Barbara who had been her dearest friend all these years. How could she feel this stab of pain over well-deserved happiness? The lines of Randall Jarrell's poem, "Next Day," came to her with sudden force, his picture of a middle-aged woman feeling gray and unnoticed, who says

"I think of all I have.
But really no one is exceptional,
No one has anything, I'm anybody,
I stand beside my grave
Confused with my life,
That is commonplace and solitary."

She let her gaze drift out to the horizon, scolded herself for wallowing in self pity, and turned to her daughter.

"Nice to see you smile, Jen. Please pass the jam."

CHAPTER 7

▼

Wednesday, February 15

Dear Juliet:

I'm sorry it's taken me this long to respond to your generosity in returning our deposit—and to your lovely note from Manzanillo. I trust you had a wonderful, healing time there with your daughters.

I'm afraid I've been caught up in this vortex of Betsy's illness and just now feel I have a few free minutes to write you a note.

Actually, I am writing this from a chair in Room 203 of Massachusetts General while Betsy sleeps. I imagine you know what it's like to catch up on your correspondence in such a setting.

Betsy is growing weaker everyday. Not only is the chemotherapy proving more debilitating than we expected, but it's almost as though she has decided that she's had enough. The other day she asked me to "just let" her go. Today she underwent more tests; the results will be in this Friday. Perhaps then we can begin to hope again. Maybe the suffering will be worth it.

My ... I've gone on longer than I think I should. Oddly, I've often thought of you during this strange odyssey. I can't imagine how you bore up for five years of seeing someone you love in such pain. "Hope is the thing with feathers." Maybe something will fly this time.

With belated New Year's wishes for you and your daughters and with thanks for your concern.

Sincerely,
Sam

*   *   *   *

February 25

Dear Sam,

I have carried your thoughtful note with me for the past few days, hoping its presence would stimulate in me the right response. It hasn't come, so I'll barrel ahead anyway.

Please just know that I empathize with you from a point so far away in miles but so close in experience. I understand your unhappiness. Please feel free to write or call if you need a shoulder. I've been there. Sometimes a stranger can provide comfort when we don't want to lean on family members, those already carrying their own grief and rage.

With wishes for some good news about Betsy.

Juliet

*   *   *   *

She dropped the letter in the mailbox in front of her home and put up the flag. She was struck by a growing sense of unease. Turning back towards the cottage, she bent to pull a weed, then rested on her knees as she saw more culprits in the flowerbeds. There was something satisfying about digging down to the root, feeling the plop of the slight yank as the offender was removed. She reached for the bucket of garden tools she kept nearby and turned some of the soil she had disturbed. Her garden was getting a little shabby. Everything seemed shabbier lately, actually. Her home needed painting, she could use a new haircut, and even Spanky could use a toenail trim.

Ever since Barbara's brunch she had been feeling low. Why? What was it? Did she think the rest of the world should share her loneliness? Was that it? Just because Barbara didn't have as much time for her, because her nights were filled (with passion, she was sure), why shouldn't they be? It was up to her, to Juliet the Brave, to find ways to have a meaningful life. Just because she couldn't seem to find a job, she shouldn't be so dead.

She should be feeling good: Jen was slowly recovering, busy with her research and friends, Tasha was doing well in her studies and planning a trip to Southeast Asia in the fall, and she was, thank God, healthy and relatively secure financially. She could wait awhile for work. She had things to fill the hours, her sewing, good books, exercise. Her house was immaculate. She had been a good wife and now she was being the Good Widow. Why did she feel so empty? Why was she so edgy?

She went inside and busied herself with preparations for yet another job interview. Being busy helped, fixed things temporarily. Her mother never had "idle hands," (the Devil's play-things, she was told) and neither did she. Paul had always begged her to relax, to smell the roses, to cease her constant rounds of activity. He saw it as a defense, a way to avoid looking at herself. Well she had time now, she was looking at herself, and she didn't necessarily like what she saw.

Dressed in her best suit and ready for the interview, Juliet looked around her lovely home. It echoed. It had always seemed so full with laughter and talk and activity. Now it was well groomed and organized, and a bit lifeless, like herself.

Her life, "commonplace and solitary."

Oh, tosh and nonsense. Just get up, put one foot in front of the other, and go to the friggin job interview, woman.

*   *   *   *

Three weeks later, still jobless, she looked in her closet for extra warm clothes, stuffed them into a duffel bag, filled a sack with 15 hours worth of Purina Dog Chow, locked the house up, put Spanky in the rear of the Jeep, and aimed her hood north. She'd think about things in Sun Valley. On the passenger seat next to her was a yellow legal tablet and a fresh Uni-ball pen, just in case she had some road-induced introspection.

As she drove into the Sunrise condo lot at Elkhorn a day later, she saw that she had filled at least five pages in wavery scribbles, most made while crossing the vast desert spaces of Nevada. The long journey had, indeed, given her time to think, and she was glad for that. Now she could afford a little space; let the thoughts sink in. As soon as she opened the door, she knew she'd made the right choice to head this way, even in the spring chill. Perhaps it was because Santa Monica had been the place where most of Paul's illness was managed, or perhaps it was because she had always associated Sun Valley with a sense of retreat, but she absolutely knew she would get some answers from being here.

She turned up the heat, gathered logs from the deck, and lit a fire. Still in the refrigerator was the bottle of wine she'd left for the Duncans. She uncorked it, poured a glass, and sat in front of the fire in the oak rocker they'd found one year on a trip to Montana. The fleece throw warmed her cold feet. It was still and peaceful.

That night it snowed, muffling all outside sounds. During the evening Juliet returned often to the rocker while she watched the flakes shimmer in the light on the deck. She felt cocooned with that great snow-silence drifting over her immediate world. She let her soul relax into it, into the comfort of safety. Wrapped in her chenille robe, meditation seeping in with the dancing fire's flames, Spanky at her feet, the remains of the second glass of wine in the glass by her elbow, she knew she would be all right.

*   *   *   *

Shaking the snowflakes off her mittens and stamping her boots, Juliet brushed her fingers against her cold doggy nose and then waved across Java at her two friends, Janice and Dottie. They motioned her over to the space they had saved for her and the "bowl of soul" they had ordered.

There is a place saved here, in this town for me. Whenever I return I feel as though time hasn't passed. I pick up the friendships right where they left off.

Now the conversation focused on her, how she was doing after all these months without Paul. They had immediately passed over light local gossip. Juliet marveled at the depth of these "part-time" friendships.

"So anyway, that was Mexico," she found herself saying after she'd brought them up to date on recent events.

"Well, I wish I'd been somewhere warm this winter, even with your traumas," Dottie said. "I'm a bit tired of the snow."

"That's because you don't ski," Janice opined. "I think being involved in a winter sport makes it more fun to live here."

"I do, too. But, remember, I work for a living. I have so much to do on the weekends, it hardly seems worth it." Dottie replied.

"Funny," Juliet chimed in. "Some people in LA live near the beach and never get there, either. Anyway, skiing sounds good to me. Anyone game?"

"I'll go with you up to Galena. I've fallen in love with skate skiing. How about tomorrow?"

"Sure. I'd love to join you. Don't you think I need a refresher, though?"

"No," said Janice. "The snow's perfect now, perfect spring skiing."

Later Juliet reflected on the ready acceptance of her women friends. One could do worse than go back and forth between Santa Monica and Sun Valley. She was blessed.

*   *   *   *

Trying to get the skate-skiing rhythm and failing, for the most part, Juliet called ahead to Janice. "Go on ahead. Don't wait for me. I'm going to rest awhile." Her friend waved, then headed on up the groomed trail.

She sat down in a small recessed area, using her parka hood as a seat, removed her skis and leaned back against a pine tree trunk. She was surprised she was so out of shape. She was breathing deeply, almost hyperventilating from the exertion. She'd have to join the classes at the Santa Monica "Y" again. She certainly had no excuse for feeling so tired.

Then she reminded herself that she'd only been back in this altitude for three days, plus she hadn't skate-skied in more than a year, so she shouldn't berate herself. Besides, one of the reasons for Nordic skiing was the chance to stop once in awhile and enjoy the wilderness. That was just what she was doing now, she rationalized. And it was gorgeous, the Sawtooths glimmering in the late afternoon sun, one peak tinged at its very top with the reflection of an impending sunset.

She breathed deeply of the icy air, closed her eyes and listened to the absence of sound: no birds, no cars, and no human voices. As much as she loved people, she craved this kind of silence. She felt happily alone for the first time in years. She'd have to do this more often when she moved here.

When I move here? Where had that come from? My home is in Santa Monica.

"Hey, Juliet! Juliet!" Janice's voice came closer. She was returning from her ski farther ahead "Get up off your buns! We'd better head back; the sun's getting low."

Juliet re-fastened her skis, stood up, waved back at Janice, and then headed back towards Galena Lodge and hot chocolate, getting the rhythm right for the first time all day.

*   *   *   *

March 25

Dear Sam:

I'm writing you from Sun Valley. I've been here since the 20th, reacquainting myself with this beautiful town. I do love it here, and find myself putting together some of the loose ends since Paul died. The first anniversary of his death is just a few weeks away. For sure I'll be back in Santa Monica by then, but for some reason I am reluctant to leave here just yet. Plan on being here till at least April 10th or so. Home for tax time.

Regards to Betsy. Maybe you'll be able to spend next Christmas here!

Juliet

The minute Juliet put the card into the "Out of Town" slot at the Ketchum Post Office, she regretted it. What was she doing, corresponding with him? She had no business inserting her cheery little self into his life. A wash of shame rolled through her. He was entitled to some privacy without being deluged with chipper greetings from someone he'd never even met! For some reason she couldn't shake thoughts of him and now thoughts of her rashness at writing him before she'd heard back from her last note. But then, she was here, not in her Santa Monica home, and so she couldn't know whether he'd written there. She was just being considerate, letting him know of her concern. Wow! She was experiencing an emotional hangover, a sign she was becoming unhinged.

On the way out the door, she saw Jerry Wells heading in. A friend of hers and Paul's, he saw her and said, "Oh! Hi. Juliet! Wait just a sec. I want to talk to you."

She loved the Ketchum post office. Since there was no house mail delivery, people stopped there almost every day. Invariably she'd meet a friend, gossip for a few minutes and often wind up going for coffee nearby. She'd been thinking about some of the people she hadn't bumped into yet, and here was one of them. Paul and Jerry had worked out and skied together years ago, forming a friendship that had survived through Paul's illness and decline. Jerry was one of the friends who had visited even when Paul was too weak to hike. Her strongest memory of the two men was seeing their silhouettes as they sat on the deck in the warm late afternoon summer sun, feet up on the railings as they looked out at golfers, hikers, and maybe even an occasional herd of antelope. These had been good times for Paul in spite of his pain.

Now she turned back into the post office and followed Jerry to his mailbox at the rear of the corridor. When he turned around, she gave him a big hug.

"Oh, Jerry! How good to see you! Do you have a few minutes?"

*   *   *   *

Over an hour later she found herself still talking to the good-natured friend opposite her. She was relating the "dating" experiences she'd had and hew new cynicism about men, especially since Tom's betrayal of Jen.

"I know you better than that," Jerry was saying. "You really don't think men are such rotters. How could you, after being with Paul for so long?"

"I know you're right. Just because I've had too many encounters of the close kind with these weasels, doesn't mean the rest of them are like that. My best friend, Barb, is with a terrific man right now, and there are people like you, good men, out there. But I must say I haven't exactly been inspired lately."

Jerry nibbled at the crumbs of the bagel they'd shared, then reached across the small table at Perry's. He rested his hand on hers, giving it a gentle pat. "Don't be discouraged, Juliet. Things'll get better. It hasn't even been a year."

She looked into his friendly brown eyes, found reassurance, and smiled. "O.K. I'll take your word for it. After all, imagine all the schlumpfs Cassie had to be with before she met you!"

Jerry and Cassie had a strong marriage of fifteen years. Juliet remembered when she'd fixed them up so long ago and reminded herself that life still held possibilities.

"Anyway, Cassie and I want you to come to dinner. We didn't know you were in town until yesterday. You'll probably find a message from Cassie on your phone machine. I have an idea I want to run by you. Can you come over tomorrow night, about 7?"

"Sure. That is, unless I meet another Paul in the next few hours." Juliet rose and hugged Jerry, who also was up and getting his jacket on.

The next night, Juliet sat at the wonderful old parsons table in the small log house out Warm Springs, sipping decaf coffee and thinking about the currents that had swept their mutual lives along. Jerry was now the director of the Medical Center's

Human Resources department. Cassie spent about twenty hours a week volunteering her time for the Advocates for Survivors of Domestic Violence, a community resource for potential and actual victims of abuse.

As always, Juliet marveled at their energy and commitment. She enjoyed them for their sense of humor, as well. Even now, they were laughing at a story Cassie was relating.

"So these darling little girls are waiting in the office and I hear one of them say, 'Let's play a game.' 'O.K.,' says the other. 'Let's play phone tag!' 'What's that?' said the first. 'Oh, you know,' the second said, 'When I call you and don't get you and you call me and I don't answer'."

"God, I love kids," Juliet said, after they stopped laughing. "I miss them, I really do."

"What a lead-in to my thoughts, Juliet." Jerry cut into a winter tart and served a slice to Juliet. "You told me you haven't found a job yet. Well, I think I may have an idea. Ready?"

"Sure. I trust you."

'Well, it's with high school kids. But maybe not the ones you were used to."

"What do you mean?" replied Juliet, savoring the sweet apples and pears of Cassie's famous dessert. "I've taught all kinds."

"Alternative school. We've recently opened one up here in Blaine County and it's doing very well. They could use someone part-time. I immediately thought of you, but you were in California."

Her interest piqued, Juliet answered, "Well, you were right. I'm not ready to do this yet. But tell me more about it."

Jerry explained that they were interested in starting a creative writing program for these kids, but that there wasn't a huge rush. He'd heard about it through the grapevine. He reassured Juliet that it wasn't something she'd have to commit to now or even for a while.

As she soaked in her warm bath that night, she remembered the good friends she and Paul had known, like John and Sally Brandon, friends from their early marriage days. The Brandons spent a summer looking for just the right apartment for them while she and Paul were on a summer trip to Greece. They had come home to the news that they could immediately occupy a freshly painted unit just two doors away from Jon and Sally's. For the next year they'd shared dinners and played bridge and, before children, lived almost a communal existence as couples. The beauty was each couple could close the doors to the privacy of their own apartments when they wanted. It had been a wonderful year. Now those were people you could count on! And so were Cassie and Jerry. Such good friends!

CHAPTER 8

▼

March 23

Dear Juliet:

I thought you should know. Betsy died last week. Her death was swift and relatively peaceful. Thanks again for your concern.

Sam

Juliet put down the letter in the pile of mail she'd just started to sort. Spanky nudged her leg, and she rose from the breakfast table where the letters were fanned out and filled his dish with kibble. Then she sat down again, looked at the date on the letter, put her head down on the table and cried. She was surprised at her grief, then realized that she was crying for all the sad people with leftover lives to kill.

Her feelings of unease at sending that note from Sun Valley had been right. He must have gotten it shortly after Betsy's death. She was ashamed of herself and sad for Sam, mixed feelings she couldn't put to rest. And the too-cute phrase "spending next Christmas in Sun Valley." God! Would she never learn to be less impulsive about writing things down?

She tried to ease her disquiet by opening and sorting the rest of the mail. She didn't succeed.

She picked up the phone and dialed Pasadena. After several rings (no phone machine on this line), a quavering voice answered.

"Hello? Hello? Who is this?"

"Nana? It's me, Juliet."

"Who? Who is this?"

"It's me, Nana. Juliet. JULIET."

"Oh, hello, dear. Just let me turn off the TV. I'm having trouble hearing you."

Juliet allowed a few moments for the ruse. She knew Nana, Paul's mother, didn't have the TV on, but needed an excuse for her poor hearing.

"All right, dear. Now I can hear better. How are you? How was Sun Valley?"

"Fine, Nana. Both fine. Listen, can I come over for a visit tomorrow?"

"What?" Nana was shouting into the phone.

"Tomorrow. I'd like to visit you tomorrow. O.K?"

"Of course dear. Come about 4:00. We'll have tea."

At 3:30 the next day, Juliet got on the Arroyo Seco Freeway off-ramp of the Ventura Freeway and then stopped at her usual florist on Colorado Boulevard. She selected a dozen pink sweetheart roses. Just short of Nana's street, she stopped at a Von's market and purchased three Hershey's Symphony Bars. She felt better already, performing these small tasks that she knew would brighten Nana's day.

She rang the bell twice and waited patiently for Nana to open the door. She heard the kerplunks of the walker before she heard the double bolt and chains being removed.

When she entered the immaculate apartment, she took in the familiar smell of Nana's place. She would always associate roses with Paul's mother. Nana's favorite perfumes had always had a rose base, and she still wore enough so that it was a consistent hallmark. Her efficiency apartment on the ground floor even resembled the inside of a rose: her Duncan Pfyfe furniture was covered in rose-patterned damask, the antimacassars were like petals, and the walls even glowed a pale pink in the dim light.

After asking Juliet to put the roses in one of her cut-crystal vases in the china closet, Nana directed her to sit down at the small dining table. The leaves for company were in storage. On the lace tablecloth was Nana's tea service and the delicate bone china she had been given as a bride in 1930.

Juliet helped her mother-in-law into the olive green-striped silk chair and then waited politely while Nana served her tea. She smiled as Nana remembered her preference for Earl Gray tea with milk, a favorite since they had traded homes one summer with a family from Hampstead Heath, about six kilometers outside of London.

Their conversation was one of catch-up, Nana asking question after question about Jen and Tasha and Mexico and Sun Valley. Juliet felt shame for her neglect in not visiting Nana more often. Her mother-in-law was still remarkably independent, even since the fall two years ago when she broke a hip and thighbone. Juliet and Paul had both been relieved when Nana was able to keep her apartment with the help at first of 24-hour nursing and now with someone staying at night. At the age of 91, she was a marvel.

"Here, dear," Nana said, reaching under the table for a large package, "I made this for you. Maybe it will help you keep warm if you move to Sun Valley."

Juliet accepted the package, opened it and found an angora afghan, crocheted in rich shades of red. She suppressed a rueful smile. How had Nana guessed one of the most important reasons for her visit?

"It's beautiful, Nana. I'll treasure it always. Yes, it will keep me warm. But it's so funny you mentioned Sun Valley. I'm thinking about moving there, at least for awhile."

"Good girl! You always had a sensible head on you. I really think Paul would approve." The elderly woman's eyes brimmed but she continued. "I think you could use a different set of horizons for awhile."

Juliet fixed her gaze on the dear face. It must be horrible to outlive a child. The order of nature was disrupted when a parent survived. Her heart pounded when she pictured the daily loneliness of Nana's life, Nana the strong woman who would never complain. Even since her best friend and next-door neighbor died three years ago, Nana had never uttered a self-pitying comment. Juliet was chagrined at the memory of her own forays on the "pity pot." Where were her guts? The women of her mother and Nana's generation were raised to accept life and its hardships in a more stoical manner than hers. While sometimes that meant living in unhappy marriages and situations, there was something positive to be said for those women. Nary a crybaby anywhere.

She took Nana's hand in hers. "Nana? If you think I shouldn't go, please tell me. I will be far away most of the year. I plan to visit as often as possible, but I won't know how often until I get a job there."

"Shush, now! The best thing for me is to know you and the girls are happy! I have my own life, so don't worry." She refilled Juliet's cup, adding just a few drops to her own. "What do you intend to do with your Santa Monica home?"

"I don't want to sell it. I think I'll rent it, first just to someone for the summer or the next few months, and then see how that goes. If I really land in Sun Valley for awhile, then I'll lease it for a couple of years. I don't want to make any rash decisions."

"Lucky girl. I'm glad my Paul saw to it that you'd be taken care of. He learned that from his father. Now you give those beautiful granddaughters of mine big hugs and kisses from Nana, O.K?"

Juliet knew the visit time was up. Odd, how Nana loved her to visit, but not for too long at a stretch. All the more reason she should have made the Pasadena trek more often.

April 20

Dear Sam:

I don't know what to say, except that I hope you will accept first my sincere condolences, and second, my apology for that silly note I wrote you from Sun Valley. I'm afraid that I was feeling so contented there that I was hasty in sending you such a cheery message. I realize now that the timing was especially unfortunate.

I guess I also didn't realize that Betsy's decline would be so rapid. I should have known better, as my unhappily required reading about cancer does tell me that ovarian cancer can be swift. In the long run, if there is anything good at all from such a devastating loss, perhaps there is some comfort in knowing that she was saved months or years of torture.

I can imagine the platitudes you are being offered. I know when Paul died and people wrote me that "it was for the best" or that Paul was "finally at peace," I cringed. I wanted him <u>still to be with me</u> but whole and healthy, of course. So know I am writing you the same kinds of inanities that people wrote me. At least now I know they were grappling with the right things to say, as I am, and that their thoughts were well intended, as are mine.

I know now, of course, that you and Betsy will not be visiting Sun Valley together. But I do hope that sometime we may meet and share further our strength and hope.

I am moving in June to Sun Valley, at least until I can figure out where I want to work and spend the majority of my time. My address is P.O. Box 3864, Ketchum, Idaho, 83340 (That's only one mile from Sun Valley ... almost the same town, really. Almost all mail in the area goes to the post office ... home delivery is rare.) Oh, and I do have a phone there: 208/622-9118.

Maybe the "thing with feathers" is the belief that we are strong enough to survive, no matter what. May you take wing in your own fortitude.

Juliet

*   *   *   *

This day was a frigid one, but Juliet and Barbara decided to walk on the beach anyway. The damp air made her friend's face even more radiant, Juliet thought, her cheeks crimson. Maybe it was just being in love. She cast a glance at Barb's bright features under the sweatshirt hood as she listened to the ecstatic details of the past few days.

"And, Juliet, he even brings me a rose every time he comes over! I know he sounds too good to be true, but I don't care. I simply don't care."

Juliet kept listening, trying to calm the tension in her stomach. Why was she having such a hard time with this? Was it because she wanted to feel the same way?

"So, we're going to Big Sur next weekend. I can't wait. We're staying at Post Ranch."

Barbara paused, looking at the quiet face of her friend. "I'm sorry I'm ranting on, but it's so good to tell someone about it. It's your turn, though. What's up with Sun Valley?"

"I think I'll leave here mid-June. Shawna Meyers knows a couple from England who would love the 20th Street place through next spring. He's a screenwriter and has some meetings set—needs to go back and forth for the next year. I'm going to start here, you know, lock up the few really valuable things and just trust they will be respectful of my home."

"Well, congrats, girl. I think this is a good move. But why wait till June?"

"Oh, I guess I didn't tell you. To honor the end of a year since Paul's death *The Clarion* is going to have a gala and do a whole-issue special on the works he did for them over the years.

I need to be here for that, and anyway, I want to spend that time with Nana. That's all the first weekend of June. So I'm kind of cleaning and organizing each day." She threw the piece of driftwood for Spanky to retrieve.

"Gee, Juliet. I guess I haven't been of much help to you. Please call if you need anything."

Yeah, sure. I don't ask things of you lately because you're always tumbling in or out of bed with Giovanni. Stop that nasty thought, girl. What is the _matter_ with you?

"Sure, Barb. Listen, you go on and have a fabulous weekend." She brushed off the sandy piece of wood when Spanky brought it to her and tucked it into the deep pocket of her windbreaker. "Give me a call when you get back. At least we can have lunch before I go." Juliet collected Spanky and got into her car. She didn't give her friend her usual hug, backed the car out of the driveway more abruptly than necessary, and sped away.

May 15

Dear Juliet:

Thank you for your recent letter. Of course I was not angry with you about your "too-cheery" note from Sun Valley. You couldn't have known that Betsy would die that week. The last letter I had sent you indicated that we were awaiting the results of tests.

So please don't ever apologize for being a sunny person. I sense that you have survived the vicissitudes of life because you have a positive attitude. Otherwise you would be wallowing in grief.

I understand the temptation to slip into severe depression over the death of a (good) mate. I am determined not to do so, but facing each day is very difficult.

I think your move, even if temporary, to Sun Valley, sounds like a good one. If it weren't for my teaching load and responsibilities, I'd be going somewhere else for awhile. Memories of Betsy are everywhere I turn. I am fortunate that my son Michael is nearby. He's been of great comfort to me these past few weeks. I imagine your daughters have similarly buoyed your spirits with their youth and vitality

As I complete these thoughts I realize that you have been especially generous in taking time to keep in touch with someone you've never even met!

Thank you for your Sun Valley address. I'd like to keep writing you, if that's O.K.

Sam

Juliet reread the last line of the letter while she sat on her back porch. The irises were luxuriant, and the back yard flowerbeds she and Paul had cultivated together for twenty years reflected the richness of mature growth. She could even smell the night-blooming jasmine, a harbinger of coming summer. She would miss this garden, her peonies, the bougainvillea lush over the redwood fence, she knew, miss the salty tang of the air from the Pacific, but this letter reinforced her sense that she was doing the right thing.

She wondered why she wanted to imprint the words, "I'd like to keep writing you" in her memory. After all, this was not a flirtation, indeed it would be inappropriate to think in terms of anything even remotely personal in her friendship with Sam. He had just been widowed, for goodness sake. They were what she thought of as situational friends; through some circumstances their lives had touched. When the circumstances changed (their mutual experience in grief, still raw for both of them), well, then, so would their friendship fade. She remembered teaching buddies who had moved away and, after a few years of Christmas cards, lost touch. She was sure that would be the same with Sam. And yet, a long absent but slightly familiar feeling crept into her heart. Whether from curiosity, loneliness, or interest, she felt a needy vague yearning. Whatever, she knew she wanted to keep his friendship.

*   *   *   *

Two weeks later, as she was putting family photos in boxes for storage, she heard a knock on the door. She hoped it might be Barbara, dropping in, as she hadn't spoken to her since her return from Big Sur. Actually, she was a bit miffed that Barb hadn't called. Was their friendship so superficial that she didn't even warrant a quick "Hello?"

Instead it was the electrician she had asked to check everything out for her renters. After all, this home was now 60 years old. She smothered her disappointment. Barbara hadn't even returned her phone calls of a week ago. She decided to take a walk over to Montana Avenue and see if there were some nice wicker pieces for the Sun Valley condo.

Outside of Twigs she ran into her friend Ramona Jones, who was stuffing fat parcels into her BMW.

"Ramona?" she called, heading toward the bright red car. "Ramona? Hi! It's Juliet."

Ramona peered from the top of her dark glasses and waved Juliet closer. "Oh, Hi! I've been meaning to call you! I hear you're leaving."

Her friendship with Ramona went back to the days when she, Barbara and Juliet, all starting out on their careers, lived in the same neighborhood. The three of them had maintained strong ties in spite of Ramona's ascension up the LA social ladder. Now possessed of a house in Bel Air and a position on the Westlake School and the Music Center's boards of directors, she still found time to include her old buddies in her plans.

"Tis true. I'm off in a few days. But how are you? What's new?"

"Oh, the usual. Olivia's graduating in a few weeks, and we're going to take a family trip to Switzerland for the summer, but ..." she paused. "Do you have time for a cup of coffee?" Without waiting for an answer, she took Juliet's elbow and guided her to Caffe' Ole! a few store fronts away.

As they sat over cappuccino, Juliet filled her in on recent events, and Ramona listened. Then she said. "Sounds great. I'm proud of you. Oh, by the way, what do you hear from Barb? I've left loads of messages on her machine. What's up?"

With an unbidden sting to her words, Juliet found herself saying, "Lots of luck! You know, she's bedded down with a Casanova from Italy. I doubt she has any time for the likes of us."

"No! God, she's had enough men. You'd think she'd be a little more careful."

"I agree." Juliet regretted her response, but, as she stirred the small demitasse spoon in the remains of her cup, she continued. "But I guess he's got something, you know, that old animal magnetism (I hear he's a real stud), and she's been man-less for a long time, so they naturally found each other."

After a few more minutes of aimless conversation, they got up, gave each other hugs and headed separate ways out the door. A surge of bile rose in her throat. She knew she had been petty and unkind in her gossip. Barbara was her closest friend, and she hadn't been charitable, had even fueled the fires of gossip behind her back. She couldn't understand why she was doing this. If she were angry with Barbara, she should have called her directly and then arranged a meeting to discuss it. She owed her friend that, at least. But instead, she had stifled her negative feelings and then let them out to a third party, even if it was only Ramona. She just hoped Ramona wouldn't tell Barb what she'd said. *Now that sounded like junior high!*

*   *   *   *

Just before she closed the doors of the bungalow for her trip to Sun Valley, Juliet returned to the bedroom she and Paul had shared for the major years of their marriage. She looked at the new comforter on the king-sized bed, and smiled. Their first apartment had a bedroom that measured only 8' by 10'. She and Paul had spent hours finding the perfect mattress and box springs, laughing as they bounced on beds in all the major department stores in Los Angeles. When they finally put their beloved bed in the apartment, they realized they almost needed to walk sideways to get to their small closet. Their room was almost wall-to-wall bed. They had had a good life in that bed and the new mattresses acquired over the years. The quilt that had covered Paul in his last months was packed away, and she had purchased fresh linens for her tenants. She hoped they would benefit from the warmth and love that this home represented.

She spotted the wicker basket with fabric and squares for her life quilt, and was glad she'd done a final once-over inspection before leaving. She needed to take it with her. Perhaps she would find a fresh subject for a square in the summer sages and trails of Idaho. Yes, she would add a square based on new memories and new beginnings.

CHAPTER 9

▼

A picnic on a lovely summer day was the perfect prescription, Juliet thought. Cassie and Jerry had once again proven valuable friends, helping her move in and then inviting her to their summer solstice party. They were seated on blankets or in beach chairs out in Corral Canyon, and though it wasn't hot, the sun had warmed their small spot by the river so that no one had yet to don a jacket or sweater.

Spanky was in heaven, running in and out of the small river, still swollen from spring rains, and the deciduous trees, the aspens and cottonwoods, had leafed out fully, so that the meadows shimmered in the slant of late afternoon sun.

Juliet felt content in a way she hadn't in the past year. She had realized that, as her grandmother had warned her, "you take yourself wherever you go," that just her presence in a different geography would not erase the pangs she felt whenever the loss of Paul came back to her. But those pangs were slightly less severe, and here the mountains provided a sense of sanctuary she needed. She and Cassie had taken a long hike this morning up one of the draws nearby, and, emerging at the saddle of the mountain, looked over the Pioneers and a vista of mountain ranges, many still capped with snow. It stirred the pioneer spirit in her, made her believe that she could keep exploring the paths of life before her without fear.

On the way back down the gully, she told Cassie all about the events just before the move, *The Clarion's* dinner in memory of Paul, the visits to Nana, how she hadn't heard from Barbara, and then related how petty she'd been. It was like a confessional, and Juliet resolved to write her friend when she got home that night.

Finally, as they turned toward the trailhead to the left of the draw, Cassie said, "Look, Juliet. You've been through a lot this past year. Don't be so hard on yourself. People make mistakes. I'm sure Barbara will forgive you anything, as long as you level with her."

Juliet took Cassie's arm in way of thanks. There was Jerry in the distance, putting corn on the cob in foil. Suddenly she was ravenous.

*   *   *   *

As she unloaded the car, Juliet intended to go immediately to her desk and write Barbara. That was the least she could do. However, as she dropped the greasy casserole she'd brought for the potluck into soapy water, the phone rang. Wiping her hands on the nearest towel, she crossed to the counter separating the kitchen from the dining area and picked up the receiver.

"Hello? Hello?"

"Is this Juliet Barnes?'

"Yes, who's this?"

"This is Dr. Nigel, from Huntington Memorial Hospital. I'm calling you in regards to your mother-in-law, Sylvia Barnes."

"Yes? Goodness … is she all right?"

"Well, all things considered, she's doing fairly well. She had a bad fall and broke her other hip, not the one we recently replaced. She didn't want me to bother you, but I thought I should. You and her son Don are listed as her next-of-kin."

Juliet felt the hot tears. *Poor Nana. And I'm not there!*

"Oh, my. Should I get on a plane right away?"

"I don't think you need to be here at this time. I've called her son, and he's arriving shortly. We've already operated, and she is recuperating. But I do think you and Mr. Barnes will have to make some decisions regarding where she goes from here."

"What do you mean?"

"I really don't think she should be living in her apartment. I am recommending a long-care convalescent facility."

"Why? She's so independent! Do you really think we have to consider that?"

"Absolutely. Her bones are extremely brittle, and I doubt that she will walk again. Please feel free to speak with me about this later. In the meantime, I will talk to Mr. Barnes about his wishes."

Juliet hung up the phone and immediately called Sue Barnes, Paul's sister in law. She said her husband was indeed on his way to the hospital and promised to call Juliet back as soon as she knew more about the fall and its long-term consequences.

Juliet sat at the counter for a minute, then went to her small slant-top desk and began writing a letter.

June 23

Dear Sam:

For some reason I feel like sharing something with you. I don't want to add to your grief, but I feel like talking to you in this way. I just received news that Paul's mother, dear Nana, fell down and broke her other hip, not the one that had recently been replaced. It looks like we're going to have to make a few difficult decisions in the next few days, as she may have to give up her precious apartment and go into a convalescent home.

This sad event has stirred up feelings in me which I think possibly are only known by those who have recently experienced what we both have. I am alternately sick for this sweet lady and also exhausted by the thought of confronting another sad chapter in my life. I'm planning to fly down in the next few days to help out, but I know in my heart that this is just another step in her decline, and I dread seeing it. She has been so strong in helping me to deal with Paul's death, and here she is now faced with the prospect of spending her last few months or years in one of those facilities she hates so.

She was so glad, if you can put it that way, that Paul could be home in his last days, and now, ironically, she probably will have no choice as to where she spends hers.

Why is this upsetting me so? She <u>is</u> old, has led a full and wonderful life, and this is all a natural process. Yet I am aggrieved for her in ways I can't express. Do you have any suggestions for me? How do we learn to accept these unhappy times?

I hope you bear with me on this (again) impulsive letter.
Juliet

As she put the letter on the counter to mail, she dialed her daughters, told them about Nana, and made reservations for a short round-trip flight to LA.

By the time she went to bed she had forgotten about writing Barbara.

*   *   *   *

The post office was crowded as always. Juliet was glad she'd taken a little extra time to spiffy up before she went to get mail, because, as she had guessed, she ran into several friends. She was surprised when she went to the counter to pay her yearly post office box fee and the clerk addressed her as "Juliet Barnes, Box 3864." How could he remember all the people who came to his counter everyday? That was one of the charms of this town. She was glad she didn't have anything to hide, because everybody knew everybody. No LA anonymity here!

She pulled her stack of mail out of the box and noticed a peach-colored parchment letter with a large scrawl, a letter from Barbara. Only then did she recall her good intentions of the night before.

When she returned home she poured herself a glass of wine, went out to the deck, and leisurely opened all her mail, saving the peach letter for last. Her heart sank when she read it.

Dear Juliet,

I was very excited about telling you some good news, but I'm not so sure now. The good news is that when Giovanni and I were in Big Sur he proposed to me! I am even surprised at myself that I am so eager to try married life once again, but I am, so I accepted. We returned to Malibu just long enough to get our passports and pack for Italy. We left two days later and were married in Venice with his family in attendance. We only returned a couple of days ago, to lots of phone messages from you, among other things. I was eager to share all the wonderful moments with you.

The bad news is that I didn't return your call first, but happened to dial Ramona because I figured it would be a short and sweet call. I wanted to save a nice long time to talk to you. But Ramona said she had spent a few minutes with you before you left, so she filled me in on what occurred that day.

I am deeply hurt that you were apparently so dismissive of me and my new love, and that you said some unflattering things about me. I don't want you to be mad at Ramona. I'm actually glad that she told me, because I had been under the illusion that you and I were dear friends. I now know I was misguided. I would like to believe that you didn't say those things, so I will give you another chance to tell me that Ramona was wrong.

I am very busy now, catching up on filming and trying to establish my new life. I assume you are also busy, but I would welcome some word from you about all of this.

Your friend?
Barb

   Juliet was deeply ashamed. She went to the closet off the kitchen, pulled out the vacuum and stared methodically cleaning every inch of the condo. This was therapy, and she hoped that by the time she was done she would be able to know what to say to Barbara. By dinnertime, she still felt nauseated. Perhaps it she slept on it, the feeling would go away.

Finally, at 11:00 p.m., she dialed Malibu, hoping to leave a message on Barb's machine. Instead, Barbara answered.

Before she could hang up, Juliet said, "Barb. It's Juliet. Do you have a minute?"

"O.K. I'm listening."

"Whatever I tell you may not make any difference, but it's time for honesty. Ramona didn't lie. I don't know whether she exaggerated or not, but the essence is that I did gossip about you. I'm so sorry, so sorry." Juliet was surprised at the tears that wet her cheeks.

"Well, O.K., I'm glad you're being honest, but why? Why would you say such things about me, and about Giovanni, who is such a dear? I don't understand."

"I don't either. I don't understand what came over me, but somehow I wanted to put down what you were feeling. I think I was jealous that you had embarked upon another great passion, and my life seems cramped beside yours. Oh, Barb, I don't know. Please forgive me. Please."

"O.K." Barbara paused, "Look, Juliet, I guess I can forgive you, but I'm not sure I can talk to you for awhile."

Juliet felt a punch in the stomach, the fist tight inside her. She didn't want to hear it but knew Barbara was at least being forthright.

"I respect that. And I understand. Please know that I have been analyzing, trying to understand the reasons for my jealousy, that it was based on feeling left out. Of course I want you to be happy. I just don't know what made me be so petty. I hope I can make amends—make it up to you somehow."

"I'll think about it, Juliet. But right now I just want to get off the phone and be with Gio, O.K.? Take care."

Juliet heard the click of the phone. She realized that she hadn't even told Barb about her flight to LA tomorrow. She still felt horrible but at least had made the first move towards some kind of reconciliation. Odd how one could think that a friend's happiness could be threatening or, worse, that someone you love should join you in your misery. The only thing she could do was wait and hope and look at her own small attitude. Maybe she could learn to be bigger than she had been then. Maybe some of Nana's generous spirit would rub off on her.

CHAPTER 10

▼

July 4

Dear Juliet

Children are dashing about me with small American flags, the smell of good barbecue fills the air, and a brass band is playing in the park bandstand only about 100 feet away. I am sitting at the end of a redwood table thinking about you at this minute. I decided to write you now, even if everyone here thinks I am anti-social.

I just have been waiting for the right time to respond to your news about your wonderful Nana, and now's the time. So here goes, even if these aren't the right words.

I think you are so upset because we tend to suffer more when those we love suffer than when we do. I think sensitive people everywhere wish the best for their family and friends. We wish them long, happy and healthy lives and, ideally, a quick and painless death at a ripe old age. When that doesn't happen, we are reminded that we are not in control. We see a child die or a life-partner in the throes of an agonizing disease, or a good elderly person made to die without dignity, and it jars our sense of what's right. It's especially difficult to accept these tragedies when they come in bunches. I, too, want to shake my fist at the sky and say, "It's not fair!" But we all know that pain is a part of life. It is life. So you want Nana to be at home in her last days. I understand. Life, though, may not allow for that. You can take comfort in her sure knowledge that she is beloved, though. How many of us know that, ever?

The dead no longer suffer. It is we, who are left with empty places to fill, who are hurting.

So all I think we can do is not dwell on the negative but do the best we can to live life as those who have left us would want— that is fully, trying to fill the empty places with good things, and with passion and joy. (I know, I know, easier said than done.)

So there are my thoughts. Please keep writing. It helps me more than I can say to hear from you and to sense that somewhere I may be of some help to you. You help me fill my empty places.

Sam

July 23

Dear Sam.

I just opened your wonderful letter upon my return from LA. We did have to put Paul's mother in a convalescent home. If I ever start whining again, please remind me of her courage and strength. She decided on her own to close her apartment and store her possessions, so she just has a few of her treasures around her, but she is not complaining. She actually reminded me before I left that the food was really quite good, and that she was fortunate to have a private room. She's determined to get around as soon as she learns the wheelchair Don brought her. Remarkable!

I hope your summer is as good as it can be under the circumstances. Are you traveling? Do you have many good friends who are there to help you through this? Are you seeing much of your sons? I'd love to hear about them.

It is very beautiful up here in the mountains. My daughters are doing well. Jen has really been brave in recovering from her broken romance; I even hear whispers of some nice young men she's seeing casually, and Tasha's just booming ahead with her studies. I am indeed fortunate.

Anyway, thanks again.

Your friend,
Juliet

August 15

Dear Juliet:

To answer several of your questions: After all these years at Dartmouth, I have many close friends around here. They have been most concerned about me, although I sense that some feel awkward around me, as if they don't know what to say or feel they can't show a sense of humor. Oddly, I want to laugh now more than ever. Summertime is here, so my closest two colleagues are away; I look forward to their return. I'm not travelling anywhere, as I decided to teach the summer session. I am booked for some lectures in France in the spring, so I'll travel then (Ah! April in Paris!)

You asked about my sons. Michael, my older son, is finishing his residency here at Dartmouth Medical Center. He and I share similar tastes in books and movies, so we exchange new books and often go to the local movie theaters together. He has been a great companion and help. Selfishly, I hope he doesn't decide to practice elsewhere.

Matthew, who is 28, has been married for a year to a lovely young woman, and they live on the Maine Coast. Incidentally, Matthew is a writer (fiction, unlike your husband's field); he's now working on his second novel and struggling. I think he'll make it, though.

Whenever I get to Maine, we try to fit in some time for sailing, one of my passions. Actually, whenever I travel, I gravitate towards water. I think the prettiest cities in the world are on bodies of water, as a matter of fact.

Betsy and I had one divergence of tastes. She was a homebody who didn't really like to travel, at least not out of the country. My chosen profession allows for lots of travel abroad, so we got used to my going alone, or occasionally with Michael or Matthew, when they were older. In all fairness to Betsy, she made coming home worth it! Anyway, we did travel to most of the national parks when our sons were young; Betsy loved to camp and turn a campsite into a version of our warm home.

So, my sons seem to have inherited my genes in regards to travel. Are your daughters the same? I've learned a bit about them, but not as much as I'd like. Please tell me more the next time you write.

I have a friend who spent some time in Sun Valley during the summer. If he is right, you must be enjoying a glorious bounty of theater, music, al fresco dining, hiking, and lots of wonderful outdoor things! He said it is spectacular there and that everything is intensified because of the short summer. You probably find that unusual as a Californian, as you are used to enjoying warm weather most of the year. But as an Easterner, I know how precious those brief weeks of July and August are. Here we start thinking of frost as soon as harvest is over. So, enjoy your lovely place.

Thanks for the reminder about the courage of people like Nana, true examples of Hemingway's "grace under pressure." We should all strive for that.

Sam

September 10

Dear Sam:

O.K. I know you just got a letter from me, the one I sent yesterday, but I just couldn't wait to send you the good news in the form of this business card. Yes, as you can see, I am now possessed of a livelihood as the assistant director of the Anton Gallery! I am relieved to be among the wage earners of the world again. Actually, I'm now convinced that it is a good thing I didn't get the teaching jobs here that I thought I wanted. It's time to do something different, especially as this is my new life! I'm also relieved to be able to work only part-time. That way I have the luxury of a flexible time and work schedule.

So I can travel to see my daughter in Santa Cruz and other friends in California if I choose. Also, I can squeeze in some time for Nana as well.

I'm not earning a lot of money, (de rigueur for a resort town, I'm told) but I like the challenge of learning about this beautiful art and seeing people enjoy it as well.

Oh. Also, I will be teaching a couple of classes for a branch of a community college, both short seminars, one on poetry and one on fabric art. Such a chance to be creative in new ways.

So, that's the latest!

Your talkative friend,
Juliet

September 25

Dear Juliet:

Now it's my turn for a PostScript: I have been forgetting, in all our correspondence, to tell you that I thoroughly enjoyed the copy of *The Clarion* you sent after the commemorative dinner. I showed it to my son Matthew the last time I visited him and we both remembered reading Paul's series in *Harper*'s several years ago about the early stages of AIDS. He was quite a journalist, and you should be proud to have shared that success with him. I especially remember thinking how good he was in his knowledge of medical terminology and, more importantly, how effective he was in translating that to a layman.

Good news from Matthew and my daughter-in-law! They have just informed me that I will be a grandfather in a few months. I am unabashedly elated over this news, tempered though it is with wishing Betsy could share it.

Sam

October 1

Dear Sam:

I think our letters are crossing, so if this is belated, please excuse. I was thinking about your comment concerning inherited traits. When I look at my two daughters, I see more of me in Tasha, and more of Paul in Jen. But what they have accomplished is that they are both doing things they want, something their father insisted on even when there were tough times.

Tasha is not that far from you, actually (I think I mentioned that she is in Boston) but planning to leave in the spring for a six month study in connection with her Ph.D. program. She will be examining how the policies and politics of the Thai government have impacted the work of relief agencies attempting to deal with the influx of Cambodian refugees from the time of Pol Pot.

Actually, I will be seeing her in November. I'm flying back to Boston for Thanksgiving with her. Jen will be presenting a paper for a marine biology seminar in Hawaii during that time (she's also chosen a wonderful field for travel), so we thought it would be good to be together in Boston.

Both girls are coming home (to Sun Valley) for Christmas, which makes me happy! Now that our Santa Monica casita has been leased until late spring, we have no choice anyway!

What are <u>you</u> doing for Thanksgiving and Christmas? I do think it is especially difficult to get through holidays, especially the first time around.

Take care,
Juliet

October 10

Dear Juliet:

I have a brainstorm. It seems a shame for you to be so close and for us not to meet. And, you would also do me a big favor in another way (more about that later) if you and Tasha would consent to being my guests at our family Thanksgiving.

It is not that far from Boston to Hanover, and I would be glad to work out the details from here to facilitate your coming to our home. My sons will both be here (and Matthew's wife, of course). We even have extra rooms to put you both up for the night or for as long as you wish. My house is a big (and resoundingly empty) old clapboard meant for lots of people. We'd love to have you join us.

If you have any extra time, I'd enjoy showing you and Tasha around Hanover and our campus. The favor: you and Tasha would add a level of interest to our dinner that might help mitigate the sense of Betsy's absence. It has been almost 8 months since her passing but this will be the first family celebration without her. So please consider my selfish request.

I will call you this coming weekend: you should have had time to read this and decide by then.

Come to think of it, I've never even heard your voice! At any rate, I look forward to doing so.

Fondly,
Sam

I've never even heard your voice.… I look forward to doing so.

*   *   *   *

"Hello?"
"Juliet, it's Sam. Oh my. You sound just as I expected."
Juliet sat on the kitchen counter barstool, taking a deep breath. "Oh? And how is that?"
"Young. I thought you'd have a young voice. Not that I think you are old. Oh, here we go. I'm putting my foot in my mouth. Actually, I figured we're about the same age. But what I mean is that I thought you might have, well, a <u>sunny</u> voice. And you do. Anyway, it's good to talk with you in person … kind of in person."
Juliet smiled. Well, he wasn't as glib as she might have thought. She liked that he was stumbling around a bit—made

her feel a little more relaxed, in case she faltered. And he did have a nice voice, deep and resonant.

"Well, thank you, I think. And you have a nice voice too, I might add." She poured some water from a bottle on the counter. "How are you doing, Sam?"

"Fine, really. Thanks for asking." He paused, and Juliet almost heard the intake of breath. "Well? Have you thought about my idea?"

"For Thanksgiving?" *Of course, dummy! Why else is he calling?*

"Yes. I hope I wasn't presumptuous. But I did mention it to my sons, and they were both receptive to your joining us."

"Good. I talked with Tasha, and her main concern was that we would be intruding on a family time that might be a bit too raw, if you know what I mean."

Juliet waited for some further sign. Then, "So. Well, O.K. If you're sure it will be O.K. with them, then, well, we'd like that."

"Great!" His voice boomed into the receiver. "This is the best news I've had in a long time. I took the liberty of reserving space on the shuttle airline from Boston. It's on me, of course."

They continued to set plans and compare events of the past few days. When Juliet saw almost an hour had passed, she was aghast at her verbosity. "Sam, we'd best call it a day … This has been on your nickel, I'm afraid."

"Worth every one, too … nickel, that is. Anyway, let's keep writing the way we have and save the conversation for the next time we see each other, in person. How does that sound?"

"Fine. I'll send you my itinerary and flight number and Tasha's phone number, just in case."

"Good idea. I'll see you soon. Oh, and thanks so much!"

"Thank YOU! Bye, Sam." Juliet replaced the phone in its cradle, rubbed her red ear, and sat for just a few minutes more at the counter. She looked at the wall calendar. October 18, her mother's birthday. How propitious. Only a month till she flew to Boston. She would always be surprised at life's turns.

CHAPTER 11

▼

On one of the last warm Indian summer days, Juliet went out to her back deck overlooking the golf course, taking her sewing basket with her. She sat in the afternoon's quiet, sipping tea and composing her thoughts. She looked at the aspen trees bordering the nearby mountain rise and appreciated their rich golden color. Soon they would shed their leaves and a winter chill would proscribe her sitting out here like this.

She had outlined a new square portraying the mountains she was planning to explore and was selecting fabrics for it when she found an envelope on the bottom of the wicker basket. It had her name on it, in Paul's handwriting.

She opened the letter, understanding as she saw the shaky script, that Paul had written it in those last days at home before he died. She felt waves of longing for him as she read the words.

My darling Juliet,

As I write this, I can picture you finding this letter and reading it. I know that you will choose to heal yourself from the exhaustion and grief of these last few years by turning to your needlework. Sometime you are bound to get down to the bottom of your basket and find this. I know it will be at a peaceful moment, so that's why I chose to hide this here.

Right now you are in our kitchen preparing me a liquid meal. I know you are doing your best to make it as tasty as the limited ingredients I can tolerate will allow. I love you for that, as I have loved you all these years for always trying to make the best of any circumstance.

I am trying to write this hurriedly, because I know you will be back soon, and I want to secrete this little missive away to surprise you later.

What I want to say to you this minute at this time of my life, which I know is ebbing away, is that I could never have expected life to be so wonderful to me as to allow you to be in it with me. You are my light and love, always.

But there's more. I came across a poem by e.e. cummings in that little book of his poems, the one you love so. Remember when we'd read the racier ones aloud to each other, especially when the girls were asleep and we had time together? I cherish those memories.

I am copying this love sonnet because I want you to accept these words as my final gift to you.

> it may not always be so, and i say
> that if your lips, which i have loved, should touch
> another's, and your dear strong fingers clutch

his heart, as mine in time not far away;
if on another's face your sweet hair lay
in such a silence as i know, or such
great writhing words as, uttering overmuch,
stand helplessly before the spirit at bay;

if this should be, i say if this should be—
you of my heart, send me a little word;
that i may go unto him, and take his hands,
saying, Accept all happiness from me.
Then shall i turn my face, and hear one bird
sing terribly afar in the lost lands.

I want you to be happy, and so I let you go into the life I am leaving.

With all my love,
Paul

She read the words two more times before putting the letter aside. Her heart was beating rapidly, and she had to take a deep breath and sit quietly for awhile before she rose and went inside.

Juliet called Cassie and asked her to take a walk with her along Trail Creek, and, as they hiked up the curving mountain path, she read her Paul's letter. When Juliet was finished, Cassie stopped on the trail, turned to her friend and wrapped her in a fervent hug.

"Oh, Juliet, don't you see? How special a man he was! He's telling you to be free to find someone else."

"I know. I don't think I would have been as generous."

"Don't give yourself so little credit. Paul loved you so much that he could invite you to be held by another man! I bet you would do the same in his place." She took Juliet's arm as they turned back down the trail.

"Facing death, I think, sometimes brings out the best in someone. At least I hope that's true. I'd hate to think that if we know we are near the end we would be our worst and pettiest. And Paul loved you enough to write this, to let you go. Do you know how lucky you are to have spent so many years with such a man?"

"I do," acknowledged Juliet. "I do."

$$* \qquad * \qquad * \qquad *$$

As she stepped off the plane at Boston's Logan Airport, Juliet felt somehow lighter than she had in many months, and there, waiting in the cavernous space by the baggage carousels, was her Tasha. In the nine months since they'd seen each other, Tasha's baby face had become more angular. Her cheekbones were more prominent, signaling a leap into maturity that made Juliet gasp. *My baby!*

On the drive back to her studio apartment, Tasha regaled her mother with anecdotes about the red tape she'd experienced in preparation for her spring assignment to Thailand. First she had endured numerous vaccinations and medical tests.

Then she'd been subjected to security checks because she would be living so near the Cambodian border. Her home would be Trat, a village not very far, as the crow flies, from Angkor Wat, the great monument to Cambodian spiritual life. Every other week she would travel by bus to Bangkok, to work with professors at Chualangkorn University. For those visits she had arranged for overnight accommodations in a guesthouse overlooking the Chaow Prayha River at a cost of only $15.00 (U.S.) a night. Her flight was booked for March 1, the hottest time of the year. Nonetheless, she reassured Juliet, "I'm young. I can take it."

She was obviously excited about her upcoming adventure. Juliet watched her daughter wind capably through the streets of Boston and wished for her all the rewards her hard work should bring. For just a few moments she wanted to be as young as her daughter again, full of the shiny promises of life. But she stepped back from herself long enough to censor the thought. She was absolutely fine at her own place and year of life. She'd had her turn at youth, had experienced its eagerness, but now it was time to appreciate her current stage of life.

Nonetheless, her daughter's hopeful anticipation was catching, and Juliet sensed a restoration of her inherent optimism. She kept this feeling through the next hours and over the day before they boarded a shuttle plane for the small airport in Lebanon, New Hampshire, where Sam would be waiting.

*   *   *   *

As they walked from the airplane to the passenger reception area, Juliet felt queasy. She realized it was because she was scared, as one about to meet a blind date must feel. She scanned the small crowd assembled inside, peering at the varied visages of men of about her age. Finally she noted a lanky man dressed in a black raincoat striding towards them. He had on a hat which partially shielded his face, but there was something familiar in his features, even from the distance. As he came closer and she heard him say "Julia? Tasha? It's Sam," she gripped her daughter's arm. When Tash, sensing her mother's nervousness, also looked toward the tall and angular figure approaching, she shuddered. For the man taking off his hat and now stopping only a few feet from them possessed a grand and crooked smile and could have been Paul's twin.

CHAPTER 12

▼

Sam peered at Juliet's face, then smiled broadly as he reached his arms forward to her. Even as she went towards his brotherly embrace, she couldn't look him in the eyes. She was aware of a strong masculine smell—not Paul's, as she half-expected, but a combination of damp tweeds and after-shave and maybe crisp burning leaves. Surely she imagined the last, but whatever it was, it was foreign to her, as was whatever brand of after shave he wore.

Tasha spoke first. "Oh, my god. You look just like my father!"

Juliet pulled back slightly, and said, "Hi, Sam. This is my daughter, Tasha, right on the button, as usual."

Tasha also went, then, into Sam's arms for a casual hug.

"Well, I can't help the resemblance." He picked up their carry-on bags and headed toward the baggage claim area. "I'm glad you're both here. Good flight, I hope?"

"Fine. It was fine, Sam."

"Sometimes those shuttle flights can be a bit bumpy, but it looks like we've got the weather on our side."

As he retrieved their two suitcases, Juliet dared to glance at this surprising man before her. How remarkable! He was almost the same height as Paul, even had a similar build. And, though his hair was thinner, it was the same rich brown, slightly flecked with gray. Thank god, she thought, his lips were a bit fuller than Paul's, though when he smiled it made her stomach crunch.

She looked at Tasha and sensed the same evaluation. She couldn't wait to talk with her daughter alone.

The journey to Hanover was peppered with the constant voice of their host. Sam told them stories about the landmarks, obviously proud of the history and beauty of this part of New Hampshire. As they turned on to the main street approaching Dartmouth College, Juliet had to agree with his assessment. The town was beautiful, obviously catering completely to the college, which served as its center. One could see the greens and the brick and clapboard buildings of the campus in the distance, and then closer as Sam turned left. They drove by a cemetery directly on the edge of the grounds.

Juliet noticed. "How interesting that the cemetery is right here, on campus. In California they wouldn't dare have a cemetery so close to campus."

"It's part of the whole picture, Juliet. Some of the first students of this college are buried here. You can see their tombstones when we take a walk later. Many of our alums request burial here, or even choose to live near the campus for the rest of their lives. Of course, almost all of them are men, since Dartmouth only recently became co-ed."

Juliet noticed students walking through the cemetery, passing graves on shortcuts to classes. What a different attitude from the fear of death she was used to. Here death seemed part of the whole cycle, accepted, not hidden away in Forest Lawns and behind large iron fences. She recalled her time at UCLA, when a visit to the nearby Veteran's Cemetery, with its long rows of identical crosses, was only done on a dare or as part of fraternity hazing.

They passed through streets lined with old houses obviously filled with college students, then came to a road winding around a pond. They turned left up one of the small nearby hills and into a long driveway lined with maples and poplars, now denuded and ready for winter. At its rise was a two-story white clapboard house with green shutters (needing paint, Juliet noted.)

As its occupants heard the motor of Sam's Ford Explorer, they emerged, two tall young men, a petite brunette woman wearing an apron, and two dogs, a black Labrador retriever and a huge and shaggy something.

"Sam," Juliet admonished. "You didn't tell me you had dogs!"

"Well, I do. You'll get to know them well enough," Sam said, as he got out, opened the doors for them and then made a series of introductions as his sons came over to the car to help with bags.

Juliet was surprised to notice that Tasha seemed quite at ease, not sharing her discomfort. She now thought that this visit was a mistake. These people didn't need to include them in this first Thanksgiving without Betsy.

After they were led to their rooms and given time to unpack, Juliet knocked on Tasha's door. Tasha was sitting in a window seat, propped up against one of the walls, looking out the window to the treetops visible from the second-story room.

"Hi, Mom. Isn't this beautiful? It's like the rooms I'd dream of as a child with the dormer and the slanted ceilings. You can tell that Betsy loved this house."

"I agree. My room is a bit more spare, but the fact that there are so many rooms in this house just amazes me. I'm not used to such space! It must be a job to keep it up!" Juliet walked over to the window and pulled over a small bentwood chair from the slant-top desk. She sat across from her daughter.

"Can I ask you something?"

"Of course, Mom. What's up?" Tasha turned her big green eyes to look directly at her mother. "Are you O.K.?"

"Oh, sure. Of course. I'm fine." She wrapped her arms around her chest. "It's just that I'm disconcerted by Sam's looks, you know, how much he resembles your dad. Were you as shocked as I was at the airport? My god, he even walks a little like Paul! And then I'm feeling a bit awkward, as though we're horning in on a private family celebration."

"Oh, Mom. It's O.K., really. As far as how much he reminds us of Dad, well, that can't be helped. That's not necessarily a bad thing. It's a little weird, but I'm already kinda used to it. And, as far as intruding on their dinner, I have a feeling that we will help them not spend as much time thinking about how Betsy isn't here."

"Well, thanks, Honey. As usual, you are wiser than your years might indicate. I'm going to get dressed and go down and help Cindy. See you in awhile."

Juliet arose and kissed Tasha's cheek; then, as she turned to leave the room, Tasha said, "Anyway, Mom, I think Sam is a smart enough man to decide whether or not this is the right thing to do. He also reminds me of Daddy because he's no dummy. So stop worrying and just have a nice time." She flashed her mother one of her most winning smiles. "If you don't mind, I'm almost done with a good book. I'll come down and join everyone in a little while."

Later, as she donned an apron to help Cindy, Matthew's wife, in the kitchen, Juliet was glad for the notion of "women's work." The tiny woman was a dynamo. Best to just help and not say too much, she thought, as Cindy handed her a potato peeler. And thank god for Tasha, who seemed to be enjoying her conversations with Sam and his two sons, sharing tales of academia over some sherry while her mom escaped to the kitchen.

"So, Cindy," Juliet heard herself say, as she gradually fell into the rhythm of the familiar peeling ritual, "Sam tells me you're expecting a baby. What wonderful news!"

"Yep. We're really happy. And the neatest thing has been seeing how it seems to cheer up Papa."

Juliet smiled. She liked it when daughters or sons-in-law accepted their mates' parents as their own. She remembered that she used to call Nana "Mother Barnes" before her daughters were born. That was the proper form of address then, but she felt relieved when she could have an excuse to be more informal with her.

She brought the bowl of peeled potatoes in water to the sink, which overlooked a big backyard lined by trees and thick hedges.

"I'm glad for all of you." She paused, trying to find the right words. "You know, I really appreciate you and Matthew and Michael being so polite about our barging in here for the weekend. I hope it is really O.K. Your father-in-law and I have been able to help each other go through these sad times, I think. But

I wouldn't want to be the cause of any anxiety or misconceptions for the family."

Cindy wiped her hand on her apron, took the bowl of potatoes and began slicing them, then layering them in a casserole with flour, cream and cheese. She let a moment or two pass before she replied.

"I don't think we're under any misconceptions. What we think is that you and Papa have had a relationship exactly as you just described it to me now. If that's the case, then there's no reason for apprehension." She continued her task, looking up occasionally to meet Juliet's eyes.

"Anyway, you and Tasha are a breath of fresh air. Since just about a year ago, when we first learned of Betsy's illness, this house has been filled with gloom. It's nice to have some new friends here. And anyway, I, for one, am glad not to have all the cooking to myself."

"Good, then. I'm glad to be of help." Juliet wiped the sink dry as Cindy put the dish into the oven.

"By the way," Cindy replied. "Sam was ready to do the cooking; he feels he can handle any of this. But I'm especially happy we don't have to be his guinea pigs!"

So far, so good. If only now I didn't have to look at Sam and imagine Paul every time. I'll get through this.

*   *   *   *

With the fire crackling in the huge old stone fireplace shared by both living and dining rooms, the quiet sounds of Satie on the stereo, and so far the conversation light and convivial, Juliet began to relax. These dear people were trying hard to make her and Tasha feel at home. Only once, when Michael had asked where the creamed spinach was, had there been any unhappy pause. He asked twice before Sam gently reminded him that no one had made it. No one had thought to prepare the dish, obviously one of Betsy's specialties. But even after that, the dining room returned to a friendly level of discourse and often animated repartee.

Michael was especially welcoming. When he asked about the kind of journalism Paul had practiced, Juliet responded, "He wrote a lot of articles for wide-circulation publications about the latest scientific and medical advances. He was especially fascinated by all the implications of developments in the applications of genetic research—you know, the ethical ramifications, the issues all of us might face in the future."

As the conversation continued with a lively debate about some recent medical discoveries, Michael interrupted. "My gosh. Now I realize. Your husband was Paul Barnes! He's one of the reasons I went into medicine. I read an article of his in *The Atlantic Monthly*, I think it was, about cloning, years before it became even a remote possibility. I was in high school, and I remember thinking that I wanted to be in medicine when some of these issues arose. I feel honored."

Juliet smiled, but demurred. "Oh, I think we are the ones to be honored. We're delighted to be here. Paul would have been so pleased that you remembered his writings."

Sam added, "Well, Michael, you don't think we'd have someone here who wasn't used to being around geniuses, do you?"

Everyone laughed, and Juliet admired how Sam seemed able to turn conversations around to make people comfortable. She also noted his impeccable manners, the skillful way he carved the turkey, the ease of his laughter.

After dinner, and Michael's insistence that he do the dishes, Sam asked if anyone would like to take a brisk walk. Juliet readily volunteered, then was dismayed when no one else did. She couldn't back out, so she gamely followed Sam outside.

At least he doesn't sound like Paul. Under the cover of darkness, it was almost possible to believe in new starts, in the ability of the human spirit to begin all over. Maybe this nice man next to her would understand her turmoil.

"I'm sorry."

"I'm sorry." They both laughed at their first words alone together since Juliet's arrival.

"You first," Juliet said, as Sam took her elbow, guiding her around the roots of a large elm near the path to the pond.

"I'd laugh at both of us, if I didn't feel so awkward. I just wanted to apologize for imposing on your kindness and asking you to come up here with Tasha. It must feel strange. So I AM sorry. It was selfish of me."

"No, don't be silly. We—or at least I—I can speak for myself—I'm having a wonderful time. My apology was for intruding upon a family occasion. I don't know what I was thinking, really. I think you all handled our being here very graciously." Juliet kept her eyes on the footpath.

"O.K. then. No more apologies. I'm just happy you're here." Sam stopped and pointed towards the sky. "Isn't it beautiful out tonight? I can't imagine why we haven't had snow yet, but at least we can walk here with ease. See the North Star? Over there?"

Juliet stopped, leaned against the rough bark of a birch tree, and took his other arm. She looked in the direction of the star.

"It's always been more than just my compass in the sense of navigation. I look upon it as a reminder that, as Whitman said,

'There's something more eternal than the stars.' I try to see it as a beacon of faith, you know, the sign of greater things than our mere existence. I always wax philosophical when I see it. Do you know what I mean?" He turned to her now, looking into her eyes.

"Sure, at least I think so. My perception is more that it is there for people all over the world to see at different times. I view it as a reminder not of our mortality but rather as, well, a talisman of the way we all live together on the same planet, under the same sky, that we shouldn't be divided so." Juliet returned his gaze.

"I like your viewpoint. I bet you're the kind of person who imagines the lives of the inhabitants of countries you travel to, rather than thinking of more abstract qualities."

"It's true. Paul was always looking at the geology of the Rockies, for example, and I was picturing the loneliness of the women who lived in the abandoned log cabins we'd come across. How funny that you sensed that." She leaned closer to him now, appreciating his wool jacket and its woodsy smell.

"It was a simple guess. I think you could be termed, in one of our contemporary cliches, a 'people person.' Pretty obvious, the way you made my sons feel at ease."

"Thank you for the compliment. Your sons are easy to be around. I really expected some kind of hostility from them. You can be proud." She waited for his response, but instead he seemed lost in thought, so she stumbled on, bringing up a new subject to fill the quiet.

"I was thinking," she said, as she looked up into his face, "that it must be a big job to take care of the house now that Betsy's gone. How do you manage?"

"Well, at least for now, I've let a few things go. I can afford cleaning help, so I take advantage of that, and I think next summer I'll get the place painted. We had planned to do it this summer, but then, well you know …" His voice trailed off. After a long few seconds, he added, "But I guess it's not that bad. I always did my share of household chores, anyway. Oh, I often cooked, did the dishes, ironed my own shirts, you know. I didn't feel that Betsy had to be my servant."

"My!" Juliet said. "Good for Betsy! I never let Paul do any of those things because I thought I could do them better, the control freak that I am! I did finally let him wash his own things sometimes. I'm sure he would have done more; he was 'liberated' for a man of his generation. But we just started out that way and never changed."

Sam smiled, looking tenderly at her. "I bet you have worked too hard all of your life. Don't you think it's time you took a rest?"

It seemed very natural when Sam took her chin in his thick mittens and, bending down, kissed her lightly on the lips. She didn't reject the kiss, rather just savored the strangeness of it, the slight taste of crème de menthe. How odd, she thought, to be kissed by someone other than Paul, to feel a different pair of lips on hers. It had been a generation since she had kissed anyone else this way. She found herself comparing the two men, almost forgetting the touch of Paul's kiss in the process. Sam's lips were fuller, as she had noted before, softer than Paul's. It felt good, but she couldn't bring herself to respond with more enthusiasm. She felt guilty, knowing this emotion was ridiculous. She needed to tuck this occurrence away and think about it before she could react properly to what was happening. She pulled back a bit.

"Sam, I ... I don't know what to say."

"That's O.K. I hope I didn't offend you by the kiss, but you do look very beautiful in the moonlight. Please don't take this in the wrong way."

"Of course not. It just felt ... different. But it's O.K., really." Juliet smiled at him. "I think, though, we'd better get back."

They walked arm in arm up the curving path towards the warmly lit home. Juliet felt at ease now, comfortable with the brief time she'd spent with Sam. She leaned against him and gripped his arm just a bit tighter as they entered the house.

The next day she was able simply to enjoy being with Sam, as she and Tasha toured the beautiful campus with him. She was most impressed with the library, where students could read in wing chairs and partake of tea. The efficient study cartels at UCLA's English Resource Center bore no resemblance to these carpeted study areas.

Sam showed them his offices in the building housing the history department. It had an extensive library of volumes about European history, several of which bore his name. She realized that part of her attraction to him was his intellect. Paul had also been very intelligent, sharp and incisive with his writings about contemporary issues. He didn't like to sit still for very long; he was always exploring and trying to discover what was around the next bend in the road or corner of a current event. His study was messy with newspapers and magazine articles, clippings from the foreign press, boxes of files filled with quotes and photographs.

This office had a different feeling, quieter, more staid. Perhaps it had to do with Sam's interest in history. One could take time researching and digging out the meaning behind events that had already happened, rather than having to accelerate one's life to find out the relevance of things happening perhaps at the very moment one was searching. By nature, Sam seemed slower and more methodical than Paul had been. Perhaps that was one of his virtues.

Why am I constantly making comparisons?

Juliet went over to the bookcases and pulled out a red leather galley proof. It was entitled *Despots to Dictators: Europe in the 1800's.* She noted the author's name, "Samuel P. Duncan."

"My. Quite a thick book, Sam. May I ask what the "P" stands for?"

"Paul." He looked at her reaction. "I know. Another coincidence. Except that no one has ever called me by that name, and it doesn't suit me. It was my great uncle's name."

"Hmm. I don't know if I believe in coincidences or not. I think we just spend our lives hurtling around and bumping in to each other in random ways, anyway. I don't think we are fated in any way to follow a preordained pattern."

Juliet fingered many of the other volumes on the shelves. "Sometime I'd like to read your books, Sam."

Sam pulled down a paperback edition of one and handed it to her.

"Here. Try out this one. I'd be very interested in your opinion, positive or negative."

Juliet took it and smiled her thanks. As they left the office, Tasha took her arm, and whispered, "Another thing Dad'd say!"

*   *   *   *

Sam drove them into Boston and then took Juliet to the airport after she said her goodbyes to Tasha.

As they waited at the boarding area, they filled the time with chitchat. Then, when the attendant announced her rows of seating, Juliet felt a surprising sense of loss. She turned to face Sam.

"Well, I've had a lovely time. We both did. Thank you for your hospitality, Sam," she said, wanting to voice something else but not quite knowing what it was.

Sam helped her with her carry-on, then swept her in his arms and whispered, "Me, too, Juliet. The nicest time since Betsy left. Thank you. I'll talk to you soon." Then, handing her the black vinyl bag, "Take care."

Now sitting in the aisle seat for the flight home, Juliet reflected on the events of the long weekend. She had definitely enjoyed herself, and she and Tasha had both expressed satisfaction with their visit to Sam and his family. She was left, though, with a nagging feeling of disquiet. She didn't know why, but decided to give her feelings some more time to be sorted. *How do I feel about him, about how recently his wife died. Should we end it here? Do I want it to end? What does all of this mean? Why do I have to analyze everything? Relax, girl!*

She ate every bit of the horrible airline food, had a second cup of coffee, pulled out the paperback Sam had given her, and began reading. At the dedication to his mentor, Dr. Gershoy from New York University, she was reminded that she had just had a glimpse into the life of a man with a totally different life experience than hers, a man from the East Coast, with an intellectual history more complex and rich than she could imagine at this time. Well, she hoped she would enjoy learning more about him. At least she could start by respecting his intellect. She could almost hear his voice reading the first sentences to her.

CHAPTER 13

▼

After unpacking her bags and starting the washing machine, Juliet sat down at the dining room table with Spanky, retrieved from the kennels and happily at her feet. First she dialed Tasha and left a message on her machine saying she had arrived safely, then dialed Jen's number. She knew she wasn't home yet from Hawaii but might check her messages, so she also left her a message.

She sorted through the mail and saw Barbara's familiar handwriting.

November 20

Dear Juliet,

I have thought a lot about our conversation. You are too special to me to let any more time elapse before I let you know I forgive you. I hope we can start again. Life is too short!

Gio and I are planning a skiing trip to Sun Valley. We won't ask to stay at your home but hope we can spend some time with you. Can you believe Gio has never skied? He's a warm weather person at heart, but I have convinced him that it's worth a try.

I'll call you soon.

Give my love to the girls. Will they be with you this season?

By the way, I did some sleuthing and found out where your dear Nana is, so I paid her a visit a few days ago. She is looking well. Actually, I'd go crazy in a place like that, but she seems in very good spirits. Her nurses say she is doing fine, has made many friends already and never complains (obviously the kind of patient they prefer). Next time you're in LA let's go see her together.

Love, Barb

Flooded with relief at the healing of their friendship, Juliet savored the letter again, reading through the part about forgiveness. Then she put the letter down, looked at her watch and, seeing it was only 8:00 p.m. in California, dialed Nana's room at the home. The phone rang several times before Nana picked it up.

"Hello?"

"Nana, it's Juliet. I just got in a few minutes ago from Boston and thought I'd check in. How are you?"

"I'm fine, dear. Don got me one of these phones that amplify the sound so I can hear you very clearly. How was your trip?"

"Wonderful, Nana. Did you have a good Thanksgiving?"

"Believe it or not, I did. Don arranged for me to go to their home for dinner … got me in a wheelchair and in a rented van and everything. It was such a lovely day."

They chatted for while, and Juliet told her mother-in-law all about the girls and the trip, leaving out the parts about Sam. She would deal with that if he became a larger part of her life and when she next traveled to California. In the meantime, she wouldn't burden Nana with any unwelcome information.

*   *   *   *

She finally felt reconnected to Sun Valley and her new life when she settled into her new routine of work at the gallery. She was glad that they needed her for extra hours during the holidays. It gave her a sense of purpose which she'd been lacking, and she enjoyed seeing the combination of locals and tourists who visited.

On this particular Friday noon brilliant December sun flooded the small gallery space with light. When she opened the blinds she was surprised to see a couple waiting at the front door. She opened the double doors and greeted the potential patrons with a broad smile.

"Welcome to the Anton Gallery. We feature artists of the Northwest. Feel free to take your time, but I'll be glad to answer any questions you may have."

She went back to the small desk at the gallery's rear wall and sat down, letting the couple set their own pace. She always felt awkward greeting people who came to view the art, didn't know why. Possibly it went back to her teenage days selling socks and underwear at J.C. Penney's. Even then, she had hated false sales-clerk conviviality and still found it difficult. She also knew how she valued her own privacy when she was in a gallery. She probably wasn't meant to be a sales person, yet in spite of her "performance anxiety," she was grateful for her employment.

As the couple expressed interest in a Seattle artist whose oils depicted the vibrant Cascade Mountains, she felt herself relaxing and actually enjoying the give and take of the exchange. While she guided them back to the spare room which housed more of the artist's paintings, she heard the front door open.

She turned around to be shocked by the appearance in the doorway of two figures, both larger than life, Gio and Barbara. She excused herself and ran to greet them.

"Barb! Gio! I didn't expect you NOW! Why didn't you tell me this was when you planned to come!" Her words tumbled out as she enveloped Barbara in her arms and then turned to Gio, tears wetting her face.

"Then it wouldn't have been as much fun, would it? We're here for a week! I thought if I surprised you, you wouldn't feel you had to entertain us as much."

"Ohmigod. Please. Take your coats off and relax. You can put them in my office back there. Let me just go check on our clients, and then I'll be right with you." Juliet waved them towards her small office space and then returned to the couple from Texas.

After they left, she leaned against the wall behind her desk and looked at her two friends.

"You don't know how good it is to see you both! I have to be here until 6:00, and then there's a special event I need to attend, but let's have dinner. Where are you staying? I have so many questions!"

She and Gio and Barbara talked for several minutes, Juliet recommending a good ski rental place. They arranged to meet at 7:00 at Warm Springs Restaurant, located by the creek. The rest of the day flew by, and Juliet had only a few minutes to freshen up before she turned her thoughts to the evening, closed the gallery and walked the few short blocks to the center of town.

As dusk fell, Ketchum shimmered. It was a tradition for most of the merchants to deck their buildings with small white lights, making the town look like the Christmas Macy's window she'd seen once in New York on a visit. Near Town Hall, several people in warm coats, knit caps, scarves and gloves were gathering outside on the curb and street surrounding a very old and large fir tree. Signs set up in front of the tree noted that the annual Hospice tree lighting was about to take place. There was a large kettle for donations, and those who had planned in advance held small candles which would adorn the tree.

Pastor Small spoke softly in the crisp air to the crowd, now numbering fifty or more people, and then began to read a list of names. Each name honored someone who was to be memorialized by the placing of a candle on the tree. Juliet listened as the names were read. Her eyes filled with tears as she saw a little girl, probably around six or seven, take a candle and place it on the tree while her father's name was read.

At least I had Paul all those years and so did my daughters. We were fortunate.

As the tree began to glow from the number of candles, Juliet was moved by the courage of those around her, also in pain. She saw her friend Emily, whose child was killed in a car accident two years earlier, and Mrs. Noble, the mother of yet another teenager whose premature death had been caused by an accident—this one because he skied into a tree on the mountain he loved. And there was Annie from her yoga class, whose own experience with devastating breast cancer and a double mastectomy had encouraged her to be a hospice volunteer, sharing her hope and care with others whose diseases had progressed to terminal stages. She thought that this ceremony was a reminder of how this town always rallied around those in need. Her thoughts were interrupted by the voice of the minister.

"Paul Barnes."

Juliet stepped forward with one of the two candles she held and placed it in the small metal holder on the tree. Then she lit it and it joined the dozens of others already in place.

As the naming of the lost continued, Juliet could almost see Paul's bright smile in the light of the candles. She felt his warmth, felt him near to her.

"Betsy Duncan." There was a pause. "Betsy Duncan."

Juliet awoke from her reverie and stepped forward with her second candle. She placed it near Paul's, lit it and stepped back. She hoped that this small gesture meant something. At least she could honor the memory of the woman she had never met and maybe in some way assuage her trepidation about her own attraction to Sam. Betsy must have been a wonderful person. She deserved to be included in this evening's remembrances.

As she returned to her place in the crowd, she smelled the familiar perfume of a friend. It was Cassie, who had come forward from the rear to stand by her.

"Juliet? Hi. I just want to be here next to you," Cassie whispered as the reading of the names continued.

"Thanks Cassie. Thanks so." Juliet let herself sink into the grace of their friendship as the choir began to sing "Silent Night." Juliet always embarrassed herself when she heard that carol. It touched something in her that triggered tears, even at inappropriate times. Now she let them flow, let them wash her clean of pain and sorrow. She let herself be restored on this cold clear mountain night in Ketchum, Idaho, so far from the life she had led, the people who had filled her days up to now.

*　　*　　*　　*

Juliet put her heavy black coat on the rack in the restaurant's foyer, let herself be embraced by the host, a young man she always felt such affection from, and then spied Gio and Barb seated by the fire. The restaurant looked out on fields of snow and Baldy Mountain, where skiers enjoyed some of the best slopes in the world. Inside, with its strings of white lights, fire, log walls and small round tables, the eatery gave off a rustic coziness, just the atmosphere Juliet was glad she selected.

As she and her friends enjoyed crab legs, ribs and swordfish, Juliet told them about the events of the past few weeks and filled them in on her feelings about the brief time she had spent with Sam.

"Well, Juliet. It seems to me that the only thing you need to consider is how much you enjoy him, not how much he resembles Paul," Gio said, while he wiped melted butter off his chin. "Life is to be lived. You've been without Paul for—how long now?"

"A year and a half," Juliet replied.

"That's a long time to be without a love. Oh, I know," Gio could see Juliet begin to interrupt, "I know that it must be difficult to picture yourself with anyone but Paul, but I don't think he would want you to be this lonely. My advice? Start to enjoy life again!" He finished off the last crab leg with elan and looked at Barbara for approval.

"I agree with Gio, Juliet," Barbara said, placing her hand on her friend's wrist. "It's time for you to think of yourself."

"That's not it. Now stop, both of you. It isn't that I'm not taking care of myself, or not allowing my emotions to be free. It isn't that, really. I even have a go-ahead of sorts from Paul."

They looked at her with some amusement, so she proceeded to tell them about Paul's letter.

"So, you see, it isn't guilt or anything like that. It's just strange, that's all. And then the problem is that sometimes Sam resembles Paul so much. I can't seem to separate the man from that uncanny physical similarity. I know that's silly, but I can't erase the feeling, at least not yet. He is like Paul in some ways, the important ones. I mean, he's intelligent, caring and considerate and generous, loves his family—all those things—but I really don't know him. He's an academic: his friends are all university people. His wife's passing is too recent. All those things make me wary. And then I think I may be imagining his good qualities because he does look like Paul. Am I making any sense?"

"Not much," said Barbara. "I think you are thinking too much. Try to relax and just enjoy the gift of this man. Take it a day at a time. That's what AA taught me. I think it applies well to all our lives. Don't intellectualize all the time."

As Barbara sipped the glass of Pellegrino she had ordered instead of wine, Juliet realized that she hadn't even been privy to this change in her friend's life.

How self-absorbed I am!

"Thank you, my friends. I'll try to remember that. But first, Barb, when did you start going to AA? I can't imagine that you were developing such a problem. Tell me all about it, if you wish."

"Not that much to tell, Juliet. After Gio and I sampled all the red wines in Italy, I looked at myself and realize I no longer had the excuse of loneliness I would pull out when I drank too much. So when we returned, I went to one of those huge Thursday night sessions at the church in Brentwood and decided to turn the rest of my life around. Gio's helped immensely."

Juliet didn't know what to say, but she knew she was proud of her friend. "Great. I'm so glad, if that's what you want. Anyway, you look wonderful, so something's agreeing with you!" She smiled and paused to sip some water. "Change of subject. Now tell me, are you planning to take skiing lessons? How long will you be here? Tell me more about what you want to do this week!"

After the waiter cleared the table and they paid and stepped out into the starry night, Juliet took Gio's arm in hers. She whispered, "Thank you for being so good to my friend, Gio. You're both fortunate." She actually meant it.

*   *   *   *

She was able to take two days off from the gallery and ski with Barb and Gio. The big Italian tackled the ski slopes with the same zest he seemed to find in all aspects of his life. By his third day of skiing, the first day Juliet was able to join them, he had "graduated" from the Dollar Mountain bunny slopes to the challenging runs of Baldy. Even well-experienced skiers felt that intermediate runs on Baldy were more difficult than some advanced runs on other mountains, but Gio was able to handle them with joy. Moreover, he surprised Juliet by being a cautious and considerate skier. He didn't get out of control and, when he thought he was skiing too fast, he came to a complete stop.

Juliet enjoyed skiing with them both. Gio entertained her by singing off-key arias at the top of his lungs while turning down the curves on Seattle Ridge or babbling excitedly over chili in the Lodge at lunch. She fully understood why her friend had fallen so in love with this vital man. His delight at the offerings of life was contagious. Juliet had more fun skiing those two days than she had had in years. She reciprocated by showing them the lively apres—ski scene and then having them over to her place for dinner as often as possible over the week of their visit.

When they left, Juliet was tired but fully assured that her friendship with the two of them was back on track.

By the time she said goodbye to Barbara and Gio and picked up Jen from the airport, Christmas was only four days away, and she had saved the tree trimming for that evening. She and Jen enjoyed "take out" from Globus Noodle and then unpacked the ornaments, talking all the time and catching up on the conference in Hawaii.

"Mom, do you know what the best thing was about the seminar?" Jen said as they worked together to string the lights.

This had always been Paul's job, though Juliet had usually bugged him to rearrange them so they were balanced with a variety of colors in each spot. She kept the old-fashioned big lights with the reflectors behind them; she knew she would never be able to have a Christmas without them. They reminded her always of her childhood and the gentle lap of her father, where she had spent so many Christmas evenings enveloped in love and magic and hope. She was unabashedly sentimental about the holidays, even when they used to be spent in sunny Santa Monica.

"No, Honey, what?"

"The feeling I got of adventure, of new possibilities. I mean, there I was in the most gorgeous weather, delivering a paper and enjoying my colleagues from all over the world. We all invited each other to visit our homes. I've got invitations to Antigua, the coast of Chile, even Australia!"

Juliet watched her daughter's cheeks glow from the recollection and from the tree lights, and recalled the wan and unhappy young woman she had parted from in Mexico when they boarded their plane just a year ago. She thanked the gods for the gift of youth and healing, then realized how much had happened to her also since that time. She stifled the impulse to remind her daughter of how unhappy she'd been only a year earlier. Instead she just smiled, pulled the stepstool over, and handed her the angel for the top of the tree.

"Mom! You always do this!"

"Not any more. I'm giving you the job. I think we should just do different things now. Oh, and I think it's wonderful that you had such a grand time. Maybe you and Tasha can meet in Australia when she gets a little time off in Thailand."

"Great idea, Mom! Let's call her, O.K.?"

They spent a busy evening finishing the tree, putting on all the worn ornaments from the girls' childhoods, the papier-mâché elementary school horsies and gingerbread men, the dough clowns, the felt Santas Juliet had made when Tasha was three. She might start a new life, but it was essential to Juliet that she not abandon these reminders of the old.

When they called Tasha she was sad she couldn't be there with them but had resigned herself to saving her money for the trip to Thailand. And, since she had just seen her mother, she wasn't too unhappy. She and Jen talked for over 30 minutes about everything that had happened, and at one point Juliet sensed that Jen was listening to a long speech from Tasha.

After she hung up, Jen turned to her mother and said, "O.K. Mom. Out with it. You haven't said anything about Hanover and Sam Duncan. Tasha tells me that you and he seemed to hit it off well. What's up?"

"Oh honey, I don't know," Juliet said, as she carefully folded tissue and put it back in the storage boxes for re-use when they took the tree down, "He's a very nice man."

"I know. Tash said so. But doesn't it feel funny to be—you know—<u>with </u>someone other than Dad?" Jen's tone was slightly brittle.

"First of all, I haven't been WITH him, exactly. I think I know what you mean by that. And, anyway, that's not really your concern."

Now Jen's eyes flashed. "Oh, really? Mom, what do you take me for? A fool? Dad's only been gone a year and a half and you fly back east to visit some man, spend Thanksgiving with him, and stay at his house. What do you think we think?"

"Let me remind you, Jen," Juliet said, with a surprising edge to her voice, "that I didn't go back to see him. I went to see Tasha and things just worked out for the extra visit. AND," she said, her voice rising now, "we were very careful not to be alone together. It would not have been appropriate. And anyway, it's none of your business what I should choose to do with my relationships."

"My mom the vixen!" Jen left the room abruptly.

Juliet was stunned. How had things gotten so negative so quickly? Suddenly she had been so defensive. The reality was that she and Sam <u>had</u> been circumspect. Maybe she was really entertaining thoughts of more and that was why she had reacted so to Jen's questions; anyway, she suddenly felt like she had betrayed Paul. How ridiculous!

She went to the guest bedroom and knocked on the door.

"Come in, Mom. I'm sorry." Juliet was sitting on the edge of the bed. She had been crying. "I don't know why I lashed out at you. Of course you have every right to be seeing someone, and even, though kids don't like to think of their parents that way, even of sleeping with someone. But it just seemed to spoil our night together, all this news. And I had felt so close as a family, almost like Dad was with us, you know?"

Juliet sat down next to her frail little bird. "I'm sorry, too. I got all defensive. The truth is that I have always loved your father and will always honor him. You must know that."

"Of course, Mom. Sure I do. But doesn't it still seem odd to even have another man near you, touch you at all?"

"The truth? Yes, it does. But one of these days I'll probably feel like being with someone in a more serious way than I have been, and I hope you will respect that."

"I do, Mom. I'm sorry. Let's go upstairs and have some hot chocolate, like we always did after trimming the tree, O.K.?"

"Sure. And I have something I want to share with you later."

On their way upstairs, while Jen went on ahead to start heating the milk, Juliet slipped into her bedroom, retrieved Paul's letter from her bedside stand, and took it to Jen's room. She placed it on her pillow. Perhaps this would help, she hoped.

CHAPTER 14

▼

It was one of those crisp January days that made skiing in Sun Valley both challenging and exciting, the temperature about 12 degrees, the sun bright, and the snow thoroughly groomed. It made Juliet wish she were a better skier, so she would feel like attempting some of the less-traveled runs, but today she was content to work on her turns and enjoy the easy glide down College run. On the way up she had had a conversation with a tourist from New York, and they had parted with the usual cliches about having a good day. Well, this was a wonderful day, Juliet thought. She could not imagine wanting to be anywhere else than on this mountain with the crystalline views, happy people and sense of fulfillment she encountered around her. She almost broke into song, smiling as she thought of Gio, making the final turn down into Warm Springs and delighting in the last smooth, straight ski to the lodge at the base of the mountain. Time for some hot soup.

She set her skis in the racks outside the lodge and, as she took a tray for the cafeteria line, noticed the man from New York just ahead of her. He caught her eye and motioned to a table piled with damp parkas. She nodded and then, a few minutes later, joined him and two other men at their table.

"Thanks for letting me join you," she said, noting that one of the faces was familiar.

As she put her tray down and took a chair, Juliet was introduced.

"Juliet?—It is Juliet, I think I remember.—This is my friend and business associate, Tom Farley," Meyers Brown said, and then nodded to the third man, "and our guide here is Justin Blake. Perhaps you two have already met."

Juliet smiled and acknowledged the introductions. "Hi, all. No, I don't think I know you, Justin. But you look familiar: perhaps from the market or post office. Are you instructing today?"

"Oh, no. I'm just enjoying myself with my friends. At least I can show them the mountain. Meyers and I go back to college days together, and I've skied with them at Stowe and Lake Placid, but this is their first time out here."

They talked for awhile about the glories of skiing and Sun Valley in particular, and Juliet felt herself sounding like someone who worked for the Chamber of Commerce.

The rest of the day she kept encountering the party of three. For some reason it buoyed her spirits. It helped her take her mind off the nagging reminder that she hadn't heard from Sam in a couple of weeks. There had been an obligatory exchange of a letter or two after her return from Boston, and they had both sent Christmas cards, Sam's with photos from Thanksgiving, and that had been it.

Now, as she gathered her mail at the post office, it hit her again. Her disappointment. Another day and no letter. He hadn't called, either. Why hadn't he called? It dawned on her that maybe he wasn't interested in her now that he'd seen her in person.

She realized that she had begun to count on his notes from Hanover, accumulating a pile she kept in her bedside table. She was acting like a mooning teenager, she thought. Well, she'd write him anyway and tell him about the terrific day she'd had. She didn't have to wait for his letter of return. That would really be immature!

After a hot bath, she checked her messages. She was happy to hear from each of her girls and made a mental note to tuck in a little extra money for Tasha in her next letter. She was due to leave for Thailand in a few weeks, and her message was filled with joyful anticipation.

The third message caused her heart to sink.

"Juliet? Hi." It's Don. Something's happened to Mom. Please call me as soon as you get this message."

Nana! Not Nana. Not now!

Juliet dialed the Pasadena number and, thankfully, heard the rich and resonant voice, so like his brother's.

"Don? Hi. It's Juliet. Tell me about Nana. I just got my messages."

"Juliet. I'm sorry, but Nana passed away this morning. She had a stroke. Thankfully she was unconscious—went immediately, which I guess is so much better than if she'd awakened to the reality that she couldn't function."

Juliet had to put the phone down for a minute and grab some Kleenex. She found herself unable to talk until she had allowed some time to cry.

"Don? I'm sorry. Just a minute while I collect myself. I do agree with you. I'm glad she didn't have to suffer. In that sense we're lucky. But I still didn't want her to go. And I wish I'd had a chance to visit her again."

"I know. But, Juliet, you were a wonderful daughter-in-law to her. Mom bragged about you to everyone in the convalescent home, thought you had such 'spunk,' as she put it. And she knew you and the girls loved her."

"Omigod. The girls! I'll call them right away." Juliet spent the rest of the conversation finding out the arrangements for the services and asking if there were anything she could do. Then she called the airlines and made a reservation to fly down to LA the next day.

She cried for several minutes, drawing on reserves of grief she thought she had emptied, before she decided to call the girls. She dreaded calling them. Their grandmother had given them unconditional love, and she knew the news of her death would be devastating to both of them. All she could do was remind them of Nana's full and healthy life and of the rightness of her going, quickly and after being ready for this "inevitable passage," as Nana had so bluntly put it when she had last seen Juliet.

"Oh, for goodness sakes, dear!" Nana had said, as Juliet fluffed up her pillow. She had just finished doing Nana's nails, one of the last vestiges of vanity still remaining in the aged woman. Juliet had been struck by her mother-in-law's thin skin, almost a bruised color, purple from the veins showing through. It was like rice-paper, almost transparent. Juliet was afraid that her fear and sympathy for Nana was just as easy to see through, just as transparent. "Don't waste any more time worrying about me. I am old, you know. It's not as though I've been cut down in the fullness of my youth or anything like that. Not even like Paul!"

The old woman had stifled a gasp when she spoke her son's name. "No," she continued. "I've led a very long and good life. I've had the love of a good man, financial security, I've lived in the best country in God's world, and my children grew up to be decent men. Now how can I complain? It's just time for me to get on with this inevitable passage."

When Juliet's eyes had brimmed with tears, Nana had continued. "Now stop that! One of the good things about being really old, like I am, is that you are allowed to say what you feel. And right now, I'm just feeling grateful that I am having this chance to let you know that it's O.K. I think God gets you prepared in a kind of off-handed or unexpected way. One day you look at that aged crone in the mirror and just think, 'Well, I'm ready.' I'm not saying I want to go this minute, but I won't be sad when it happens. Look at all the good people I'll get to see again."

And Nana had rested back on her pillow, folded her arms and given Juliet an almost naughty wink! What a lady!

Juliet wished she were possessed of that kind of faith. But even if she weren't, she'd have to be strong enough to call the girls.

*   *   *   *

Juliet, Tasha and Jen stayed in Malibu with Barbara and Gio during the three days she was in Los Angeles. She bought a ticket for Tasha even though Nana would have thought it foolish and frivolous for the money to be spent on flying just when she was about to embark on her adventure. Juliet found solace and comfort in being with her daughters and Paul's family and in her friendship with Barb and Gio, but she was glad when she unlocked the door of her Sun Valley home. She thought if she had to hear "Amazing Grace" one more time she would collapse! She could use some normal time, just living without airports and drama and sadness. She yearned for a few weeks of a relatively boring existence.

She was thus surprised at the leap her heart took when she opened a letter from Sam that had arrived in her absence.

January 9

My dear Juliet:

I have waited several days to write you because I wanted to work this out very carefully before I wrote. I have been thinking of you all the time since you left, but I have needed to sort out these unexpected emotions. First I felt guilty for finding someone so attractive to me so soon after Betsy. Then I remembered how much she had reassured me that it would be O.K. if I fell in love again. But more than those two conflicting feelings, I was possessed of the vision of you as also a very vulnerable person who had worked hard to begin a new life. It may be selfish of me to interfere in any way with the progress you have made on being an independent and contented person.

But I've decided to hell with all that wondering. Carpe diem and all that stuff! What I propose is this: I am going to France in April for a conference at the Sorbonne, and here goes. Will you join me? I realize this is a big invitation, but it seems a shame to waste that time. I think I would spend those days wishing you were there.

Of course I'll cover all expenses, including separate rooms should you wish. I always have been known as a gentleman, and I don't choose to change that aspect of my character now.

Let's get to know each other on long strolls by the Seine and slow dinners over French cuisine.

Please let me know what you think about this.

I'd love to show you the Paris I love.

Fondly,
Sam

Juliet wrote back immediately, even before she unpacked.

January15

Dear Sam:

Your letter caught me as I have just returned from Los Angeles and services for Nana, who passed away last week. You can imagine my state of exhaustion and my state of mind.

My answer? Of course. Let me know where and when and I'll be there. Springtime and Paris and the company of a good man sound like heaven.

I'll write you more in a few days when I get my life back on keel.

By the way, how is Cindy? Isn't she due soon?

Fondly,
Juliet

January 21

My dear Juliet:

First, let me say how saddened I was with your news about your dear Nana's death. I know how much she meant to you. Please accept my condolences. I won't burden you with cliches about the blessing of a quick death, etc. I know it still hurts, no matter what. I am thinking of you. We have both had too much grieving, I think, and hope we can turn our thoughts to more happy events.

As for me, I'm doing well, thanks in part to you. How wonderful it was to hear that you will go with me to Paris! You have warmed the cockles of my heart, to cite a venerable old saying! I now find that the heavy snow that recently fell on Dartmouth is not unwelcome but glimmers in its crystalline beauty in a way I'd forgotten. I walk home by drifts of the heavy stuff and don't even grumble. Instead I find myself singing and smiling like some madman in the Steppes of Russia. If you rent *Dr. Zhivago*, you'll see what I mean. I'm not Omar Sharif, but you are as lovely as the young Julie Christie in her ice palace.

So I honor you from so far away. I hope you have lots of time to ski. I'm afraid I have tabled much skiing this season (perhaps a few days at Stowe) because I am having a very busy term here and because I want to use my spare time to visit Matthew and Cindy. Regarding my work load, it is onerous. I am completing the draft of a new study of the Bolshevik Revolution (hence my absorption with Siberian winters, I guess). I would like to complete it before I go to Paris. And, of course, I need to work on my presentation for the seminar there at the Sorbonne. And, in addition, I have a dynamo of a research assistant who is keeping me on my toes. He is maybe too vital for me! Not to mention I have some of the most wonderful students I've encountered in years (adding girls was a real boost to the dynamics of academia here) and I don't want to give them short shrift, so I keep revising my stale lecture notes, trying to find more exciting ways to present history. It all adds up to an exhausting semester. But you have given me new purpose and zest. Thank you!

As far as Cindy, well I must tell you she is radiant, albeit in the even-more-cold-than—New Hampshire Maine winter. I drove through sleet and snow like the postman to see them over New Year's. It was worth it. I love the concept of being able to see pictures of the baby in utero. We certainly didn't have those treats, did we? I remember being banished from the labor room when Betsy delivered. Now Matthew, like so many young men, is going to be there through the birth. Michael is planning on assisting, too. What a joy for all of them! Matthew, like his Pa, seems inspired by his personal life and has got his book at a publisher. He's working with a difficult editor but learning a lot. The baby's due in late April, so all's well.

Enough for now. I will call you in a few days just to check in. In the meantime, I will arrange everything for the trip.

To Paris!

Love, Sam

CHAPTER 15

▼

So here she was, headed toward Paris with this tall man in the seat next to her. The weeks had passed so quickly that she still had to remind herself that it had been over four months since she had said goodbye to Sam at Logan Airport. Nana's death, her days at the gallery, letters back and forth to New Hampshire and Thailand, skiing whenever she could find the time—all these had made a blur of the time between her acceptance of Sam's invitation and the actual boarding of the plane.

The hostess offered them drinks, and Juliet accepted a glass of red wine, as did Sam. They toasted each other and sat back in the business class seats. Juliet averted her eyes from Sam during her first few sips, feeling suddenly shy. *I should feel this way. I'm heading towards Paris with a man I hardly know! Do I feel a connection with Sam simply because I need a man next to me? Is it because I feel comfortable with him with his reminders of Paul? Is it some kind of transference? How can I trust my feelings?* She hated herself for her constant questioning, the way her analytical mind went round and round in these circular arguments. She would have to learn to trust her feelings more, just let things happen.

Juliet placed her hand on Sam's arm and let it stay there until he took her hand in his, and they both remained quiet with their own thoughts. She was aware that they were taking a big step. Paul had now been gone two years, Betsy one, and she knew this was the first time either of them had contemplated actually being intimate with another partner. She felt a joyous crunch in her stomach at the thought of being with Sam and let herself decide to live the next few days as though she were young again, ready to embark on an adventure. She would try to leave any emotional baggage back at home.

The flight had turned out to be full of conversation. She began by talking about her admiration for Sam's book.

"I loved your book. I found it very provocative, Sam. You write about complicated things with such clarity. It reminded me of the way Paul tackled medical subjects." She sipped the red wine and nibbled a cashew from the assorted nuts the hostess had offered them. "It helped me understand the background for some of the events of the 20th Century, the rise of the Bolsheviks, the advent of the World Wars. You made the 19th Century interesting!"

"Thanks. I hope my students feel the same way."

"They should: I think they're lucky. But isn't it hard to appeal to this generation? I mean, the relevance of 19th Century European history to kids who've grown up in a time of such invention and development?" Juliet was enjoying the chance to have an intelligent discussion with Sam.

"Don't forget. I've got the cream of the crop at Dartmouth. But I know what you mean. When I was a student, there just wasn't as much to learn. So sometimes I think that current events take precedence to "ancient" history. The explosion of information never ceases to amaze me. Actually, I admire this new generation. They have to wade through so much!"

Both passed on the movie, preferring to talk and talk until the plane set down at Charles de Gaulle Airport. Sam enjoyed pointing out some of the landmarks of Paris on their taxi ride from the airport. Images from the books of Collette and her favorite Truffaut films came to mind, along with all the wonder she had thought might disappear with age. Here she was, at last in Paris! She relished taking it all in. By the time they arrived at the charming Hotel de Lutece on the Ile St. Louis, Juliet's fears were calmed. She could be herself with this man.

Sam spoke fluent French to the desk clerk, and Juliet knew just enough of the language to understand that Sam had arranged for rooms next to each other on the same floor. She was relieved and yet slightly disappointed. She knew that sooner or later they would want to share the same bed.

After Sam tipped the porter he followed him to the door, checking his watch.

"It's 1:00 P.M. Paris time. Why don't I give you a chance to take a nap or bath … deal with jet lag, O.K.? I've made reservations at a nearby restaurant for 9:00 for dinner. That way we can both have some time to unwind. I've got some calls to make about the conference, anyway. I'll check with you later, say about 4:00. If you need anything, though, please don't hesitate to call my room or knock on the door."

He left, a grin on his face.

Juliet looked around at the small but comfortable room with its cherry wood furniture, rough cream-colored stucco walls, and aged wood beamed ceilings. They were on the top floor. The bed, a double, had a wool blanket and simple, clean linens. She went to the window, threw open the curtains and looked out at the narrow street below. The afternoon sun slanted off the gray stones and copper roofs of hotels and residences across the way. Not far away she could see the spires of Notre Dame.

On the small table next to an upholstered chair she saw a bouquet of fresh tulips and irises, a bowl of fruit, and a bottle of Perrier. There was a note. She took off her shoes, poured a glass of the water and sat in the comfortable chair, then opened the note.

To Juliet:

I hope your stay will be as lovely as you are. Sam.

Her heart leapt again, and she carried the glass and the note over to the bed where she unbuttoned her skirt and nestled into the deep pillows.

What a beautiful start. I couldn't ask for more.

✻   ✻   ✻   ✻

When the phone on the bedside stand rang, Juliet jolted up. Who could that be? Where was she? She picked up the receiver.

"Juliet? Hi, it's Sam. Are you O.K.?"

"Oh. Sam. My god. What time is it?"

"Seven o'clock. I didn't want to disturb you. It was so quiet in there. Did you rest?"

"Did I rest! I must have fallen asleep soon after you left me. I had a sip of the Perrier, read your note and sat down on the bed. And here I am, almost 5 hours later!" Juliet realized with a start that her bags were still sitting unpacked. Never in her whole fifty-plus years of life had she ever not unpacked immediately upon entering a hotel room or upon returning from a trip.

"Well, good. I'm very glad you rested. I did too, as a matter of fact. I made my calls and closed my eyes for awhile. How soon shall I gather you up?"

"I haven't even unpacked. Can you give me about 45 minutes? I'd like to take a bath."

"Sure. I'll be over then."

"Oh, and Sam, thank you for the lovely fruit and flowers and especially for the note. See you soon!"

Juliet took out her clothes and hung them in the small closet, glad she had thought ahead to pack a wrinkle-free black dress and cashmere sweater. She luxuriated in a bath, fluffed up her hair, sprayed on some of her Tiffany perfume, put on pearl and diamond earrings and a brighter lipstick than usual, checked herself out in the mirror above the small dressing table, and was ready at almost exactly the moment she heard Sam's knock on the door.

She almost saw a blush on Sam's smooth cheeks when he took her arm.

"You look beautiful, Juliet."

"Thank you. I think the nap helped!"

"I hope you don't mind if we walk to the bistro I chose. We have plenty of time, and it's only a few blocks from here. The evening is so clear I thought you might prefer it."

"Sounds wonderful!" Juliet leaned against him as they walked along the small interior street of the Ile St. Louis. They turned onto the Rue St. Louis en L'Ile, and Juliet noted the charm of the old buildings and street lamps.

"It's hard to imagine that I've never been to Paris! Paul and I traveled, but somehow never got here. We were saving it for a nice block of time after the girls grew up. We saved it too long, I guess."

Stopping at a corner under a street lamp, Sam said, "That's too bad. You would have had some wonderful times here together, I'm sure. But as long as you haven't been to Paris before, I can be especially proud to be the one to show you this magnificent city!" He actually picked her up and twirled her around, setting her down gently. Juliet was surprised at the sensation of feeling like a teenager.

"And here's our first treat. This is one of my favorite restaurants."

Sam ushered her inside the restaurant, called Chez Henri. He shook hands with the maitre'd, and they were led to a table midway through the restaurant along the wall and near the bar. From this vantage point they could see everyone who came in. When she looked around her, she noticed that all the patrons seemed to be French. At least there weren't any obvious tourists except for the two of them. Paul conversed casually with the waiter, then turned to Juliet.

"What would you like for starters? I would recommend their escargots. They're sinful!"

"I'm going to be very old-fashioned and let you do all the ordering. I'm liking the feeling of letting you be the leader here. You know the restaurant, the language, the city, so, please just surprise me."

As they savored the meal, Juliet's admiration for Sam's sophistication and knowledge increased. He was courteous and charming to the waiter and, it appeared, knew the subtleties of the cuisine and the language. He seemed truly at home, and she felt herself reacting to his worldliness by falling into a long-forgotten attitude.

She remembered when she was a girl going out with her first "college" men, thinking them so witty and masterful. As high school seniors she and her closest friend had attended a fraternity party at U.C. Berkeley with her cousin and his best friend. They had giggled at the luau's signs that referred to getting your "leis" here, equating ribald humor and the drinking of alcohol with charm and manliness. They had been in awe, feeling lucky to be with "older men." And here she was, thirty-five years later, feeling the same girlish admiration.

This time, though, her increasing excitement was based on elements she hadn't experienced in a long time. Being in a foreign city with a man who could function well in that world—a man whose attention was focused on her pleasure and enthusiasm—was flattering. She enjoyed letting him take over, enjoyed feeling like a young girl with a crush again. It was O.K. to throw aside her independence and need for control for these few hours!

After dinner they took a different route back to the hotel, along the Seine. Leaning against the stone railing wall, absorbing the sensations around her, the smell, the taste of old, mellow cognac still on her tongue, the sounds of a cabaret from a far street, even the chill of the cool April air, Juliet felt the magic of Paris rush into her. She was amazed that Sam had had the discipline to wait until after dinner to walk this way. How worth it this was, though, with the reflection of the lights of the city on the famous river. Across the river they could see Notre Dame by the moonlight.

She couldn't resist telling Sam about her special connection with Notre Dame. A few years ago, she ran into an old sorority sister while marketing in Brentwood. The woman, Sue Ann Thomas, looked shocked at seeing Juliet, and then told her that she had received an alumni pamphlet recently, updating alumnae. In it, next to Juliet's name, was the letter "D" for "deceased. They had laughed at the time, but in the next few weeks Juliet had received many letters from friends saying they were relieved to hear that she was still among the living! One of them was from a devout Catholic friend who lived in Paris. She noted that she had been lighting a candle in Notre Dame for Juliet ever since she read the booklet.

"So I wrote her back immediately and asked her to keep doing so, as I figured I needed all the help I could get!"

Sam roared. "What an experience. I suppose you already knew the line of Mark Twain's when a newspaper erroneously reported his passing."

They said it simultaneously, "The reports of my death are greatly exaggerated!"

They both laughed. Juliet said, "Oh, sure. I used that incident for a long time to liven up dinner parties."

They were quiet for a few seconds. Juliet had a catch in her voice when she broke the silence. "Truly, though, I can't imagine anything more wonderful than being here right this minute in this beautiful night with the Cathedral under moonlight. Just standing here is almost too much to bear!"

She turned to Sam and looked up at his Paul face.

Sam lowered this face closer to hers and asked, "I'm glad you like it."

"Oh Sam," she replied. It's perfect. It's what I have always dreamed it would be …"

Before she could finish, Sam kissed her. This time she let herself truly feel his lips, feel the emotions surging within her, feel the need to be cherished and fulfilled, at least for these few moments. They kissed a long time, and Juliet let herself melt into his caress, wanting not to stop.

Soon Sam pulled away slightly, saying, "Let's go back to the hotel."

Juliet nodded, feeling herself spinning, a bit dizzy from the cognac and the kiss and the wild beauty of the night, and they walked almost timidly arm in arm until they entered the hotel. Once inside they went up the elevator without speaking.

When they stopped in front of Juliet's door, Sam said, "Would you like to come in for a nightcap? I have a beautiful view. Would you like to see it?"

Juliet said, "No nightcap for me. I feel a bit tipsy. But, sure." She saw that his room was much bigger, with a somewhat larger bed. It was at the front of the building.

Sam went over to the drapes and opened them as Juliet followed. "Here is a view you can't beat. Voila!"

Spread out before Juliet was a cityscape, Paris glittering over the Seine! So Sam <u>had</u> deliberately led her around the other side of the block of buildings across from the hotel, to save the river's glory for the end of the evening.

Sam came up behind her as she looked at the view, handed her a small crystal glass of water, and then stood next to her as they looked out over the city. Juliet could feel his breath so close to her, inhale his masculine fragrance. For more than a moment she yearned to be held by this man.

After a pause, Juliet said, "Oh, Sam! Thank you. I'll never forget your treat. I'll never forget this evening and you."

But as he turned to kiss her again, she said, "But I have to go. I'm just not ready. Can you forgive me?" She couldn't look at him. She felt overwhelmed and afraid and sick to her stomach. *Why am I feeling like this? What is going on?*

As she turned away, heading for the door, Sam stopped her. *Not again. Please, not another nasty scene!*

"Juliet, Juliet. Please stop for just a moment. I'm the one who got us separate rooms. Please." Sam's voice was gentle. "I don't want to have anything happen between us that isn't your choice ... or, actually my choice, too. I don't want you to be with me if you aren't comfortable. So, please. Let's call it a night."

"Thanks, Sam." Juliet said, as she let him lead her to the door.

"Don't worry. Nothing's been spoiled. Look. I have a meeting at the Sorbonne with the conference people at 10:00 in the morning. It's not far from here, maybe 8 or 10 blocks. It should be over around 11:00 a.m. I'll come back and then we can have lunch and plan our day. My first lecture is scheduled for 3:00 and then I have a surprise planned for the evening. Let's just rest and not worry about anything."

"O.K., Sam. I'll be here at 11:00 or so tomorrow morning. Good night.... and, thanks again."

When Juliet got into the small bed alone, she thought about the recent incident. Thank god he was a gentleman. She wondered what had possessed her. Would she ever feel a normal set of emotions about a man again?

She really wasn't sleepy after her long nap, but after she had read for several minutes, she turned out the light and willed herself to sleep. She finally fell into a deep sleep and dreamt of Paul as the young man she first saw at UCLA so long ago.

From her deep reverie, she heard knocking. The rapping intruded upon the sound of the waves crashing against the Malibu shoreline of her dream, and it took awhile to separate them. She sat up in the hotel room bed. The sounds continued.

"Just a moment," she called, slipping out of the covers and into a silk kimono she had left at the foot of the bed. She called out again and then asked, "Who is it?"

"Juliet, it's Sam. Are you O.K.?"

She went to the door and opened it just far enough to see Sam standing there, fully dressed.

"Oh. Hi. What time is it?" She pulled the kimono more snugly around her chest and brushed back her hair.

"It's 8:00. I have to get going," but I'm just checking to be sure you still planned to meet me when I return this morning."

Juliet was suddenly embarrassed at her state of dishevelment, didn't want those merry eyes twinkling at her any more.

"Of course. I'll meet you at 11:00, as planned. Have a good meeting this morning!"

Juliet closed the door and immediately headed for the bathroom, where she showered and brushed her teeth, aware for the first time in a long while that someone had seen her as she looks in the morning. She'd been able to take that for granted in a long marriage, but here she was, as this late stage of life, having to think about her appearance at odd times. She hoped she had the energy for romance!

The little things of her new life still surprised her. For example, she thought, while the hot shower water soothed her lower back, she couldn't remember when she had lost track of the time of day. It was almost a joke in her family. Paul or the girls could ask her what time it was, and she always was accurate within five minutes without ever looking at her watch. And she had never needed an alarm clock. Something always stirred her out of sleep at almost exactly the time she had determined she should awaken. And now she'd lost rack of time twice in her brief stay in Paris! What was happening to her, to her orderly manners?

By the time she went downstairs, it was almost 9:00. It was drizzling slightly, and she asked the desk clerk to recommend a good neighborhood cafe. She tried out her college French and, in spite of a smirk from the waiter, was served a good thick cup of coffee and Prolain bread. She sat at the small iron table and looked at the Parisians on their way to work as they walked by the cafe. She observed the style of the women: she'd always read about their sense of fashion and elegant carriage. Her expectations were confirmed by just this brief glance at the working women of Paris. She hoped it would clear later today so she would be able to sit outside and people-watch again.

She filled the next two hours by walking around the neighborhood, stopping at a newsstand to buy *The Herald-Tribune*. She entered a small church and noticed the rows of candles. She lit two of them and left an appropriate donation in the vessel nearby, then stepped out into the bright sunshine. On the way back to the hotel she saw a flower stand and couldn't resist buying a lavish bunch of violets and then a bouquet of lilies of the valley for her room. The delicate white blossoms reminded her of her mother, who had loved them, partly in tribute to <u>her</u> mother, who also had loved them. A legacy of flowers, in effect. Gardenias and roses were also her mother's favorites, and some of them always graced the coffee table of their home in the crystal swan dish whenever they were in season. She still couldn't smell gardenias without remembering the masses of them at her mother's funeral, mixed memories, really. Flowers, beauty and sadness seemed intertwined.

She was visited by a pang of bittersweet emotions. April was the time of renewal, springtime, and hope and yet also the time when she could easily fall into a sense of loss. She had attended Paul's funeral just two Aprils ago.

These maudlin feelings vanished when she opened the old French door to the hotel and saw Sam there.

"Ah, Madame, you look lovely!" he said, as he arose from one of the chairs in the lobby and strode towards her. He kissed her hand. She couldn't remember when anyone other than Paul had thought her lovely. Sam had called her that twice in 24 hours. Time to return to the present.

CHAPTER 16

▼

Sam asked the desk to have the maid put Juliet's flowers in a vase in her room, and then ushered her into the now bright Parisian day. As they crossed over to the Left Bank and hailed a cab, he told her about his meeting and she summarized her morning for him. Any tension as a result of last night's ending seemed to have vanished. It only crossed her mind once, and then only as a reflection of the absence of any negative feelings.

The taxi pulled up to a small side street paved in cobblestones.

Sam took her elbow as they walked down the street filled with small jewelry and antique shops. At each window, Juliet stopped, marveling at the exquisite displays. She suddenly wanted to buy everything she saw, amazed at her greed.

At one leaded-glass window, she saw a pair of earrings that captured her mood. She pointed out the red crystal dangles to Sam. They were the color of burgundy wine reflected in firelight. Before she could object, Sam took her in the shop and, in quick French, had them taken out of the window. She tried them on and turned tentatively to Sam.

"Well?" she said, with a coquettishness that surprised her.

"Spectacular. Just a moment." Sam went over to the counter and engaged in a short but slightly fervent conversation with the jeweler. Then, turning to Juliet, he said, "Sweets for the sweet. They're yours. Now we'd best get to lunch. My meeting's not that far off."

"Sam. You shouldn't have. I hardly know what to say." Juliet stumbled through her thank yous. She took the earrings off and put them in the exquisite little leather box the jeweler had given Sam, then tucked them in her purse.

A few doors down, they entered a small "super marche" where Sam purchased some Roquefort and Camembert cheese and then went next door to a boulangerie and bought a loaf of crusty French bread.

He said, "I thought we'd have more time together if we just lunched in the sculpture garden along the Seine. By the time I get you back to the hotel and then take the Metro back to the Sorbonne, I will be cutting my time rather close."

When they settled on a bench along the Seine, Juliet prepared their lunch. Handing a hunk of the aromatic French bread to Sam, she said, "I have a better idea. Why don't you just get the Metro directly from here and I'll stay here in the gardens for awhile longer. I think I am capable of walking back to the hotel. I saw a couple of things I'd like to buy the girls back in one of those shops, and anyway, it's a beautiful day. I promised myself more people-watching."

Sam smiled. "O.K. It's nice to know you can look after yourself during my meeting. Oh. And maybe tomorrow you'd like to come with me to the university. I think you'd enjoy the milieu, and the people watching there is wonderful!"

They enjoyed their savory lunch and talked about the beauties of the day. Sam looked at his watch a few times, and finally said, "It's 2:00. I'd better go. I need a little time to prepare and also want to be there early enough not to insult my colleagues." He rose from the bench, gave Juliet a brotherly peck on the cheek, and left.

Juliet enjoyed the peace of being alone. It crossed her mind that developing a relationship took effort. While she had enjoyed being with Sam, she was also perfectly happy here watching children on swings and slides in the pocket playground, noting how the children caught balls with their feet, soccer-style, feeling the warmth of spring sun on her cheeks, just being quiet for a few moments.

Nonetheless, she got up after awhile and returned to the earring street, as she would forever remember it, where she bought a delicate bracelet for Jen and an antique ring for Tasha. Now she felt like a bit of a tourist, but reconciled that with the memories she'd have every time she saw those baubles.

She walked for awhile along the Seine, appreciating its day life, then hailed a cab and returned to the Hotel de Lutece. In her room there was a message from Sam:

My dearest Juliet:

I asked the concierge to slip this note in with the flowers, as I assumed you would be here before I returned, and I just wanted to remind you that I have a surprise planned for this evening. You might wish to have some of the fruit, as dinner will be rather late. Would you meet me downstairs in the hotel lobby at 6:30? This should give you time to rest.

Sam

Juliet felt the now-familiar pang of anticipation. She pulled the chair over to the window, then sat for a few peaceful minutes looking at the late afternoon sun reflecting over the rooftops before running herself a hot bath with some drops of perfume added to the bubbles. She took out the red velvet dress she had packed at the last minute and then opened the leather earring box. The earrings were a perfect match.

When she descended the winding stairs to the lobby, she saw him at the far end of the lobby and, carrying a light coat and her purse in her arms, entered the room, her heart fluttering.

He arose, kissed her hand, helped her into her coat, and escorted her out of the hotel. They walked short while to another small hotel on the Ile St. Louis, and there passed through the small lobby to the bar. They settled into a corner booth lit by a beveled glass wall sconce.

She slid closer to him, liking the plush fabric and his proximity. He smelled of a subtle after-shave, one she could not identify. He leaned over and kissed her cheek.

"So. You look gorgeous. Red is a wonderful color for you." He paused, signaled to the waiter, and then took her hand in his. "And the earrings are perfect. Somehow lush and vibrant, like the woman who wears them."

She felt an electric rush from her toes up.

"Thank you for the compliment. I love them. I went back to the shop later and got the girls a couple of things. I had a wonderful day … how was yours … how did the lecture go? Who else was on the program?" As usual, she felt herself talking too much, asking questions and running on before they were answered.

Sam told her about his afternoon and then, when the waiter appeared, ordered drinks and also a plate of olives and pistachios. He turned to Juliet.

"That's not much. I hope you're not famished. We're not eating till much later, and I didn't want you to be hungry during the opera."

"The opera? Oh my! We're going to the opera?" Juliet could only hold his hand tighter and look into his eyes. She thought she was blushing like an idiot.

"Yes. We're going to the Opera Bastille. I hope you like 'Cosi fan Tutti.' And then we'll dine later at another one of my favorite spots."

In response, she leaned in even closer to him and kissed him. She didn't even care if anyone thought it unseemly, two people of their age, acting like young lovers.

Later she would recall the evening's spell, which started by listening to Mozart's music in Paris' austere new opera house. Then they had gorged themselves on oysters at Bofinger, where Sam had reserved a table in the Grand Salon, which was enclosed by a magnificent floral glass ceiling. The night was full of sensory delights and was, indeed, one of the most enjoyable she had ever experienced, certainly since Paul had become ill seven years before.

During the opera she kept looking at Sam and the uncanny profile so like Paul's. She couldn't edit the thoughts in her mind, comparing the two men as she had already done too often. As she stole glances at him, she felt ill at ease. He wasn't Paul, couldn't be, and yet his appearance took her up short. She realized she wanted him to be Paul. She had to put those thoughts aside if she were to embark on this new relationship, and during one of the more vibrant arias of Act II, she was able to table the debate in her head and be carried away by the beauty of the music.

During dinner they had held hands across the table between courses. By the time they returned to the hotel, Juliet felt entirely natural walking to Sam's room with him.

This time, as soon as the door shut, they were in each other's arms. For the first time in years, Juliet felt herself slipping into a sensual mood where she could not worry about being in control or about anything except the reality of her feelings at the moment.

Sam kissed her, and for just awhile she forgot to compare his kiss to Paul's. Sam let her free for a few moments. He slipped off her coat and took it and her purse to a big wicker chair, then returned to her and looked carefully into her eyes.

"Juliet? Is this all right? I want you to be sure."

"Yes, Sam."

He guided her to the bed, where she leaned against it while he carefully removed her red dress and then her bra. She sat down on the bed, suddenly shy again. The unbidden thought of her appearance surfaced. She was over fifty, for god's sake. Did she look O.K.? At the same time, Sam walked over to the lamp and turned it off. He seemed to sense her timidity.

"Is that better?" he said, leaning over to her and gently placing her on the bed.

In response, she murmured, "Thank you." Then, when he had taken his clothes off and slipped in next to her, she felt it necessary to elaborate: "Sam. Thank you. I feel somewhat awkward, you can understand … new man in my life, and all. And then …" she gulped at the frankness of her statement, "I'm suddenly feeling self-conscious about my body, my age, you know." *There goes this romance.*

She felt him move towards her. He took her in his arms and held her closely. "Oh, dear Juliet. I should have known. Of course. But you are beautiful. Don't you know that? I don't want to be here with anyone but you. I'm with you because of everything you are—everything your years of life have given you. And, by the way, your body is just fine with me. I can wait to see it in greater light when you are more comfortable."

And, as she felt the warmth of his body next to hers and as he began to kiss the back of her neck, then place feathery light kisses all over her face, Juliet did indeed feel beautiful. She forgot to analyze anything, just fell into the giddy spell of his attentions.

✳   ✳   ✳   ✳

The nightmare was so vivid she could smell the musty dirt of the cemetery, feel the chill of the night air on her face. Two graves were disturbed, and as she stood by, one of them erupted like a small gray and ashy volcano and thrust a coffin out. Then the lid began to open. Paralyzed, Juliet could not bear to see its contents, but, as though mesmerized into a state of passive acceptance, she watched the body emerge. The flesh was beginning to deteriorate, so that only half of the cadaver's face was recognizable, but its identity was clear enough. It was Paul! There was Paul, turning his half-face towards her. She noted with horror that he was grinning, but the broad smile she had loved now resembled a large wound, a terrifying grimace. She screamed as the corpse began to climb out of the coffin and move towards her. In her dream she screamed, the screams echoing.

For the third time since she had come to Paris, she awoke in a disoriented state. She tried to shake off the nightmare, then glanced at the sleeping figure next to her. *Paul! Thank god, Paul is really here. It's O.K.!*

Juliet reached over to the strong shoulders, and moved her body closer so she could be with him, cradled like the two-spoons position they had always assumed before going to sleep. She put her arms around him. *Paul! I'm safe.*

But the man wasn't Paul. He smelled of a different after-shave. He wasn't snoring, his skin was of a different texture, and, as she cradled him in her arms, she noted that his chest was not matted with thick hair as was Paul's. *Sam! Omigod, it's not Paul. It's Sam. It will never be Paul again.*

She pulled away, tasting the salt of tears, crept out of bed as quietly as she could, slipped the red dress over her head, gathered up her things, and left the room.

After she entered her room, she checked her watch for the time. It was 5:30 a.m. She took a hot bath, then packed her things and sat down at the small table and wrote Sam a note.

Dear Sam:

Please forgive me once again. I'm afraid I can't explain what has happened to me. Please just know it has nothing to do with you. You are a charming, vivacious, gallant man, so kind and considerate of me. I want you to know that our night together was wonderful—all of it. My leaving has nothing to do with that. I will always treasure every moment of our time in Paris. But I have to go. I can't even explain it to myself. I just know it's not fair to burden you with my anxieties. Have a beautiful time while you are here.

Please forgive me.

Love, Juliet

She read the note once before putting it in an envelope, realized it was wordy and repetitious, and thought, *To Hell with it. He's not grading it. I can't explain anything more.*

Then she picked up her bags, looked around the small room to be sure she had everything, walked out the door, slipped the note under Sam's door, and took the elevator down to the lobby.

She returned her key to the desk clerk and asked him to book her on the next flight back to the United States.

She left Paris at 9:00.

CHAPTER 17

▼

Crocuses and tulips had come up in the beds surrounding Anton Gallery, the trees in the southern part of Blaine County had begun to leaf out, and Juliet was finally aware of springtime. The gallery was only open four days a week, which gave her extra time to live with herself, something she was not sure she wanted to do. She tried to take daily walks with friends and keep in close touch with Tasha and Jen in order to feel anchored.

One day, walking by herself on her lunch break, she ran into Justin Blake, the skier she'd met on the mountain several weeks ago. He had then walked her back to the gallery and, while admiring the choice of artists represented, asked her if she would like to take a walk with him the next day. As they drove about 50 miles south to trails finally getting dry enough to traverse and then spent the day exploring the Camas Prairie, they discovered they had much in common. Both of them loved dogs and the outdoors and were relatively late arrivals from big cities. Justin was from Seattle and still maintained a home there, though he seldom returned. At first his visit, like those of so many Sun Valley residents, had been brief, for skiing in the winter or kayaking in the summer. But, as was true of so many others, he found it increasingly difficult to return to the city, even though he loved it. Now he viewed vacations as visits to Seattle, while his real life was in Idaho.

On their next walk they brought along their dogs, who got along famously, as dogs do. Juliet asked him some personal questions and found out he was divorced (twice), 49 years old, younger than she, and had one son by his first marriage, who was now 25 and a geologist. He had invested early on in Microsoft, knowing several employees of the wonder softworks company, and was now feeling blessed that he could live on his dividends and do what he really wanted.

They became platonic friends. Somehow this new focus helped her avoid her self-loathing about her abominable behavior in Paris.

She had received three letters from Sam, but hadn't the courage to write him yet.

The first, written from the Hotel Lutece, was brief and just acknowledged her departure and said that, of course, he forgave her. The second was truer and more painful.

April 25

Dear Juliet:

I am writing you from the private retreat my study at home has become in recent months. I am able to think more clearly, for some reason, in this space. And I certainly need clarity at this juncture.

I am disappointed that you didn't stay on in Paris with me. I felt that we had experienced a remarkable closeness and actually slept so soundly after our lovemaking that I didn't even hear you leave. I awoke at 7:30 and called your room. When there was no answer, I knocked on your door. Finally I called the front desk, and they informed me that you had just caught a cab to the airport.

Without trying to add to any negative feelings you may have about what you decided or about me, I must be honest. I was sick over your leaving. I'm sure if you had just told me what was bothering you, we could have dealt with it, as we did about your leaving my room the night before. I only want you to be comfortable. I need to understand if I did something to alarm you or insult you. Was I not a considerate lover? If so, you gave me no clue at the time. I am sitting here feeling quite inadequate, really. Please take the time to write me and let me know what I did, so I can deal with whatever flaws I need to root out of my character.

On the other hand, please know that those two days in Paris were marvelous for me. They will remain in my memory as a sign that life can be lovely and loving and meaningful for me once again. I just wish I could think that you would be willing to remain part of that picture in the days ahead.

You are a beautiful woman, Juliet, kind, sensual, and dynamic. Any man in the world would be proud to have you on his arm.

My arms feel very empty right now.

Love, Sam

When she read the letter, Julia was immobilized for several minutes. Sam's words made her think about how she would have felt in his position. Imagine taking a supposedly mature woman to Paris, wining and dining her, waiting patiently while she exorcises her demons, you think, then finally make beautiful love with her, only to awaken to her sudden absence. In his place, Juliet could only imagine the feelings of rejection. They must be enormous, especially without an explanation. How would she feel if he had fled from her bed after their first night of intimacy together? She knew she would think that she was somehow repulsive or that he had realized he really didn't care for her. All her fears about her fitness and attractiveness as a woman over fifty would have been reinforced. How could she let someone she cared about go through the same distress?

And then, the first week of May, there was a third note:

Dear Juliet,

You may be beyond caring, but I wanted to share the good news with you. On May 1, at 3:00 a.m., Cindy gave birth to my beautiful granddaughter. Her name is Elise Betsy Duncan. I'm driving over this weekend to see my precious gift. Since you and Cindy seemed to get along so well, I thought you'd want to know. Mother and daughter are fine. Michael got to deliver her. Papa and Grandpa are ecstatic!

Sam

Juliet didn't know what to reply to Sam, so she procrastinated. *Just what you did with Barb, you wimp.* She did send a small cross-stitch sampler to Cindy and Matthew with the baby's name and date of birth. She spent her free time talking to Jen on the phone, catching up on her reading, and writing long letters to Tasha, whose adventures in Thailand were aptly recorded on the small blue airmail letters arriving from Trat to Sun Valley every few days. Jen had arranged to go to Australia in June, and Tasha would fly there from Thailand for a four day rendezvous, so their conversations were full of plans for the upcoming trip.

Finally, one evening in the second week of May, during a phone conversation with Jen about the financial stretch of Jen's trip, Juliet heard herself (yes, the overly cautious Juliet who had obsessed all her life about frugality) say, "Listen, honey. Life is too short. This is a wonderful chance for you and Tasha to spend a few days in a place you may never see again. Once you've settled into life's routines, those chances fade. Go for it!"

"Thanks, Mom. That makes me feel a little better!"

"Well, as your friend and mine, Barbara, would say, there is only today. We should relish every moment of happiness that is offered us. So relax and enjoy. I wish now that your father and I had done some of the things we always talked about."

After hanging up the phone, Juliet was struck by the hypocrisy of her words. Not only had she not seized the day when she was in Paris but she wasn't even taking care of today's essential business, business that was ruining her serenity. She needed to call Sam right now and let him know that it was her phobias, not his lack of prowess, that had ruined their time.

She dialed his number but got no answer. She left a message on his machine.

Two hours later the phone rang. With a mounting sense of fear, she picked it up.

"Hello?"

"Juliet. It's Sam, returning your call."

"Oh, Sam. Thank you for calling. I'd understand if you never wanted to speak to me again."

"Oh, come on now. Why would you think that?"

"Because of the way I just vanished like that. And because I haven't written you or answered your letters. Because I'm such a wimp." Juliet found herself crying again. *Damn it! Why couldn't she control her crying?*

"Stop. Stop now. Take a breath. I called you back because I'm willing to listen ... and because maybe what you will say might help me out of the funk I'm in." Sam's voice broke slightly as he said these words.

"I understand. First, though, tell me about Elise. How big is she? Did you get over to see her? How did the labor go?"

"She was 6#, 10 oz., has lots of brown hair. She's gorgeous. The labor was relatively short, I'm told, about 7 hours. But that's not what I'm in a funk about. That and my work are the bright spots. It's the other thing I can't shake."

Juliet took out a peanut butter square from the candy jar on the counter and nibbled.

"Sam? Sorry for the pause. I just took a bit of candy. Courage food." They both laughed. "Anyway, here goes. About Paris. I still can't quite figure out what happened, except that I had a horrible nightmare about Paul rising out of the grave, and when I awoke and reached over to you I thought for a moment you were Paul, that you had never died and were with me to make me feel safe."

"Oh, Juliet, darling! How awful! I would have listened, I would have comforted you. Why did you run away?" Sam's voice was soft.

Juliet fidgeted with the candy wrapper. "I still don't know, except that it wasn't from you. I realize now that I wasn't running from you. Please hear me on that. You were wonderful. I had a really wonderful time."

As Sam listened to her ramblings, it occurred to Juliet that indeed she hadn't run away from Sam, but from Paul's ghost. How could she put it into words?

"So, I think I just didn't want you to be burdened anymore by being with someone who still has so many ghosts, who couldn't see you for what you are but hung on to an image of you as an echo of her life with Paul. Your resemblance to him doesn't help."

"Juliet. I think I understand. And I am somewhat comforted by the idea. But as long as we're being honest, may I tell you something at the risk of hurting your feelings?"

"Sure. That's the least I deserve." *Here it comes. He never wants to see me again. I'm hateful and unworthy.*

"It's not meant to hurt you but to put things in perspective. Do you think I have been with you without thinking of Betsy? Do you think you are the only one with ghosts to contend with, or, as my sons would say, nightmares in their closets?"

"I hadn't even thought of what you were feeling. Pretty self-centered." She tore the candy wrapper in shreds, took out another piece and popped it into her mouth while he continued.

"Well, O.K. This is what I was feeling. Your shade of lipstick the first night in Paris was exactly the same as Betsy used to wear. Red was her favorite color, too. When you chose the red earrings it crossed my mind that I would have been buying the same jewelry for Betsy. When we made love I had to consciously erase any memories of the touch of Betsy's skin from my mind. I willed myself to concentrate on your uniqueness and only-Juliet beauty."

Juliet gasped.

"I'm sorry. I would never have told you such things, but I think I need to be really honest with you, have things out in the open. I have my ghosts, too!" Sam's voice had risen.

"Ohmigod. Sam! I'm sorry. I hadn't even thought of your feelings. I was just so caught up in your physical resemblance to Paul that I didn't even imagine that you might be experiencing memories or doubts. Please forgive me for my selfishness."

Sam's voice was calmer now. "It's O.K. Do you understand what I mean?"

'Yes, I think so." Juliet paused. "Where do we go from here? Is there anywhere to go?"

"I don't know. I have a suggestion. Let's call a moratorium on letters or phone calls for a month. That will give us both time to sort out our feelings about what we've experienced. And I do think this is a case where time will do some healing. How does that sound?"

Juliet caught herself sighing. A month without contact? "Actually, Sam, I have a thought. On June 10, let's each sit down and write a letter to the other and express our feelings, what we think about the whole thing. And then we'll talk, O.K."

"Fine." Sam said. "But to make this even, let's both open them the same day. Promise that if you get the letter before the 15th you won't open it. We'll both open them on the 15th and then plan to talk, no matter what the outcome. I'll call you at 7:00 your time on the 15th."

Juliet smiled. Leave it to Sam to provide some color to the event! She was bound to have drama in her life, even if she tried to run away from it!

"Sounds fine. Talk to you then. Bye. Take care."

"You, too. Bye."

CHAPTER 18

▼

May 17

My Sweet Tasha,

First, let me respond to your recent letters. It sounds like you are learning so much! I couldn't believe the description and photos of your little house. How you can function so well with such a minimal of creature comforts is a tribute to your father's genes! You know me … I love to travel, but we're talking car camping at the roughest. I can't imagine living with a bathroom that consists of a porcelain hole in the floor (your thigh muscles must be getting strong from squatting) and a barrel of water that you replenish once a day. Well, you're young and brave and on an adventure. I take it back: I could probably live with the minimal accommodations, but not the bugs. Do you have a mosquito net? Please take some pictures of your bedroom.

I was glad to hear that your research is going well, though it must, indeed, be very frustrating to deal with the bureaucracy. I guess that is one of the things you are learning about your chosen area of study. If you keep wanting to be employed in the world of foreign affairs and at the same time "do some good," in other words, implement programs that will have a positive effect on the countries you serve, you will probably encounter lots of resistance and red tape and engage in the kind of soul-searching you are doing now (i.e., what are the long-term effects of our policies, do these people really need us here, etc.) I'm glad you are keeping the ramifications of the whole third-world/ the-U.S.-as-rescuer problem in mind.

I'm so proud of you—but then I always have been!

Life here is plodding on. As you requested, I have invested your share of the small inheritance Nana left you and Jen. When you return in October we can take care of all of that. Jen seems really happy. I am envious of your plans to see each other!

I have been putting in lots of days at the gallery. Anton is traveling in the Caribbean at the moment, so he asked me to cover. We are gearing up for the end of "slack.' The reality is that most of the galleries are open for shorter hours than usual and won't resume full-time schedules until the Memorial Day weekend. It's pretty quiet here. Having never lived in a seasonal place, I find it strange that restaurants close for slack, but the truth is there just isn't much business from the closing of the ski mountain (Easter, usually) through April and May. So it is very quiet here. I have some days when I see only two or three customers.

Thus, I've been catching up on my reading. Do you want me to send you any paperbacks? Let me know … I've read some nifty ones lately. Also, I have finished two more squares of my life quilt, one with the sages and greens of Idaho (there are tiny people hiking in the foreground) and another honoring Nana, full of the rose colors she loved. It's of two women having tea together, kind of like her elegant table. Every time I look at it I think of her and her skills of endurance combined with her gentility. I miss her more than I would have expected.

Enough of my sadness. And a personal note. Sam and I are going to think about our relationship and get back with each other in a few weeks. I'm sure you don't want to hear the details, but I just want to reassure you that he and I both respect our relative grieving periods and want to be very careful that we honor our past lives as well as our present concerns in maybe starting to spend more time with each other. I don't know how I really feel about all of this, but he is such a gentleman and I trust his instincts on this completely. By the way, he's now a grandfather! Cindy had a baby girl on May 1—name is Elise Betsy Duncan—he's thrilled, of course.

The trees have bloomed and riots of tulips are in most gardens in town. Now I understand why spring is such a joy. I was glad to put away my ski boots for hiking boots, though the trails are still very wet. At least I can take Spanky for long walks. He's in heaven!

I love you, honey. Don't worry about writing too much if you're busy. I assume you are keeping a journal which you may want to share with Jen and me later.

Kisses and hugs,
Mom.

Juliet sealed the letter and marched across the street from the gallery to the post office to get the correct postage. Standing in line, she spotted Cassie waiting for a package, and projected her voice across the space. "Cassie! Hi, Cassie!"

Cassie turned around, and smiled. "Juliet! Hi! I'll wait for you outside."

When Juliet emerged into the bright spring sun, she saw her friend over by a small card table where a tall man in a baseball hat was seated, his back to her. He was speaking to Cassie about a petition on the table and, as Cassie leaned down to sign the papers, he turned his head. It was Justin. She realized she hadn't seen him for several days.

He arose and said, "Hi, Juliet. It's good to see you. I just persuaded your friend Cassie to sign this petition about eliminating some of the dams so we can get our salmon back. Can I get you to do the same?"

"Sure." Juliet picked up the pen from the table and signed the papers without even reading them. "I trust you to be involved on the right side of the issues, and if Cassie agrees, well, then that's enough for me."

She turned to Cassie. "I've got to lock up the gallery, but then I'm free. Do you have time for a quick latte?"

"Sure. See you at Java in about 10 minutes?"

They parted and Juliet returned to the gallery, gathered up her bag and purse, set the night alarm and walked to the coffee house. She ordered her latte just as Cassie came through the door. She took the coffee to one of the wooden café tables and waited for her friend to join her.

Cassie joined her shortly. Both women took deep breaths, sounding like sighs, and then laughed simultaneously.

Cassie said, "My! It sounds like we have the cares of the world on our shoulders! I feel like we haven't talked in ages. What's new?" Her words tumbled out.

"Lots and not much, at the same time." Juliet found herself spilling out everything about the Paris trip, then about meeting

Justin. Her friend listened eagerly, nodding often and encouraging the torrent of words with "ohs" and "yesses."

"So that's that, Cassie, except I'm a bit confused at this time." Juliet sipped her now-cool latte and continued. "I haven't even asked about you and the house. Is it done?" Cassie was due to move into a new log home north of town sometime soon. Juliet had admired the patience with which she and Jerry had withstood the delays in construction, especially with a long winter, the moving of deadlines, and the time needed to do much of the finishing work themselves. They deserved the relative luxury of their new home.

"I guess that's why I sounded stressed. We're moving next week! Please plan on being our first house guest. Would you like to bring Justin? He and Jerry know each other, you know. Please say yes. It'd be fun."

"On one condition. We bring the dinner! You will be tired enough from moving." Juliet started to gather her things, then stopped and said, "Oh gosh! I forgot. I'm driving to California over Memorial weekend for a few days. My tenants are leaving and I need to clean up the house and prepare for renting it again. Anyway, can we do it the first weekend in June? You'll be more settled, too."

"Of course!" Cassie said. "Just let me know if it'll be one or two of you."

Later that evening, on impulse, Juliet called Justin and invited him to go to Cassie's when she returned from California. He accepted with pleasure.

*   *   *   *

Memorial Day was overcast, as usual, a reminder of summer mornings at the beach before the fog would burn off and brilliant sun emerge. Juliet breathed the salty air deeply, reveling in the moisture, hoping her skin would soak up some of the humidity after being parched by the high desert suns of Idaho. She had missed the ocean, missed the feel of sand beneath her toes, the sight of seabirds flying, the space of a horizon having no visible end. Just being here, at Barb's, on her deck with a hot cup of espresso and a day ahead without any immediate responsibilities, was satisfying beyond what she could imagine.

Odd, how the attainment of a sense of peace, how feeling serenity in the simplest of settings, could be so rewarding. As a young woman she spent wasted hours regretting the unplumbed choices of her life. While she had adored Paul and their life together, she had often let a thought of an imagined life on the stage drift in to her mind while changing a diaper. Sitting with other young mothers in a park watching their children climb slides or play in the sandbox, she could feel her thoughts stray from the conversation about toddler discipline to fancies about dancing by the Aegean Sea in a taverna lit by Chinese lanterns. She acknowledged her wanderlust when she daydreamed of Africa during those early morning hours spent wading through her students' weekly compositions. Even as she wrote her summary comments, being sure to include a positive observation about the paper, she was seeing zebras and gazelles in the veldt.

Well, she hadn't traveled all those places, but she had learned to love the places she was in, like this one. How could anyone not feel fortunate to be sipping coffee while wrapping the sensations of the Pacific around her? People traveled miles to vacation on beaches even less beautiful than this one, flew hundreds of miles to ski the slopes of Sun Valley. She lived in both places!

Barb emerged through the sliding glass doors of the breakfast nook with a fresh carafe of coffee, and Juliet accepted her offer of a refill. Barb sat down in the redwood lounge chair next to Juliet. Both were quiet, savoring the coffee and the moment.

Barb broke the silence.

"So. Did you sleep well?"

"Sure. The sound of the waves crashing was quite a soporific. I'd forgotten how soothing that is." She sipped more of the flavorful Italian roast espresso. "You know, Barb? I've missed this, the freedom that the space of the ocean gives, walking on the beach, being near you. I love the mountains, don't get me wrong, but I think I've got Southern California in my bones."

Barbara looked into her friend's eyes and, now pouring another cup for Gio, who was coming towards them, said, "So what does that mean?"

"I don't know, to tell you the truth. In many ways I feel now like my home is in Sun Valley. I don't want to lose that wonderful warmth I feel there. And yet ..."

"Well ... do you have to make any kind of decision now?"

"Only about the Santa Monica house. Since my renters have left, my options are open. Look at me!" she said, rising to be greeted by Gio's hug. She sat down. "You'd think I've got some big tragedy in my life. Instead I'm presented with such lovely options.... whether to live in Sun Valley or Santa Monica. Poor me!"

Juliet gave the comments a sarcastic edge and continued. "Gio, I was telling Barb that I have really missed the ocean. So I have some decisions to be made."

"Well, cara mia, it seems easy. Live in both!" Gio's voice boomed across the quiet morning air.

"Believe it or not, I've thought of that. It's just that the income from the rental of either place provides a nice style of living for me."

"So the question is, do you have the financial freedom to keep both places open for you to be in whenever you choose?"

Again, Juliet was struck by the silliness of her debate. People were starving and looking for a simple roof over their heads, and she owned two homes outright. How much she could now appreciate Paul's foresight!

"Well, thanks, Gio. I'm thinking about that. Right now, though, I'm going for a quick run on the beach. Anyone want to come with me?"

Both Gio and Barb shook their heads "no." As Juliet felt the damp sand firm under her feet, she looked back at the two of them, chairs pulled up right next to each other, and waved. The bright image of the loving couple stayed with her as she headed towards Point Dume. She made a mental note to applique a pillow for them depicting the two of then together on the deck.

She ran for almost an hour, her calves pulling against the unfamiliar tug or the sand. She occasionally ran into the fine edge of white left by the breaking waves, displacing sandpipers who were busy flirting with the sea. By the time she returned to the gray wood beach house and her two friends, she had made a decision.

*   *   *   *

The party swirled around her, the smells of the lamb shishke-bab and hamburgers on the barbecue, the shrill cries of children playing in the sand or exhorting their parents to come in the water with them, the civilized chit-chat of the guests on Barb's deck. The sun had come out. Now, at about 75 degrees, the day had sparkled and set an almost perfect holiday scene.

In the midst of all the gaiety, Juliet experienced a pang of loneliness. She felt more alone than she had in a very long time. She tried to pull out her feelings, look at the reason for the disquiet, and then be able to put it to rest so she could enjoy the moment, this beautiful place, the interesting people, but she couldn't. Maybe she was missing her girls. She decided to see if she could at least talk to Jen, but found herself frustrated when her daughter didn't answer the phone. She was probably also at a party. She couldn't talk to Tasha, either. It was now such a widely different time zone in Thailand, and Tash didn't have access to a handy phone. She couldn't ever seem to find a time to call when one of them wasn't sleeping!

She realized she was lonely—lonely in the midst of plenty, lonely in spite of a vivacious host and hostess, lonely in spite of the multitudinous mixture of voices around her. She missed … Sam! Then it hit her. She wasn't missing Paul, but Sam. Or, rather, she knew she would always miss Paul in many ways, but the empty space in her heart since his passing was being taken up by thoughts of Sam. This concept was too much for her to absorb, so she shook off her mood of isolation, got up from her perch on the deck railing, and carried her iced tea to a cluster of guests, one of whom she knew.

She introduced herself to the rest and settled into the bland repartee of large parties. She deliberately feigned interest when the conversation turned to new cars. When asked what she drove, Juliet easily said, "Oh, I've got a Jeep. It's great for the trips between here and Sun Valley." Part of her hated herself for wasting even a few minutes on such superficial and "can-you-top this" comparisons, but knew also that she needed to take a breather from the kind of introspection she had been wallowing in.

Later that night, in Barb's cozy guest room, she was refining her list of things to do tomorrow at the 20th Street bungalow. Her long list was quite ambitious, but now she could cross out some of the items she had written down earlier in the week when she was planning her trip to California. She reached deep into her large canvas carry-all, found the red Uni-ball pen she preferred to use for bank account reconciling, and crossed out "Call broker." She looked farther down the list and edited out another, "Replace items for new tenants?" "Sell odd furniture." also was eliminated. None of these would be necessary, at least not until another crossroads in her life. For now she wouldn't rent her home: she wanted to know she could come home here if she needed. As long as she had the best of two worlds, she would enjoy them. If her financial situation changed and she had to choose, she would do so then, but not now. There were more important steps to take in her life. She couldn't wait to go home in the morning.

As she turned out the light and closed her eyes, willing her tension to be erased by the rhythms of the waves crashing on the shore, she let her mind wander into a mantra of sorts, in synch with the roar of the ocean. It was Sam, not Paul, Sam not Paul, Sam, not Paul. *I missed Sam this afternoon.*

CHAPTER 19

▼

Juliet enjoyed adding some of the decorative items she'd packed in the car when she closed up her California home. She was surprised at how good the wooden toys Paul had made looked on the mantel in the Sun Valley condominium or how a few albums of family photos made her feel more at home in the large living room. She was glad now, for her decision, would plan to stay at 20th Street sometime this summer. She was happy she could feel free to go there whenever she chose. Just knowing that made her feel more contented in this mountain space, less claustrophobic.

One of the first things she did after putting away her clothes and loading the washer was to call Cassie at her new phone number.

"Hi! Cassie. It's Juliet. How are you?"

"Fine, great, in fact. I love my home, can't wait for you to see it! Are you still planning on Saturday night here for dinner?"

"Of course. Listen, I want to try out a new recipe, so please let me bring the food."

"O.K. Oh, and Juliet, Jerry ran into Justin the other day. He said you'd included him. Is that right."

"Yes. I'm looking forward to it."

$$* \qquad * \qquad * \qquad *$$

The following Saturday night Justin picked her up at 6:45 and they drove the 10 miles out of town into the area known as Eagle Creek. There they turned up a canyon now filled with expensive homes, driving past them until the last available private land before the U.S. Forest Service boundary.

And there it was, the home that Cassie and Jerry had designed and saved for for over ten years. Cassie greeted them at the door, took their coats and the dish Juliet had brought and led them into her living room, a comfortable, unostentatious space with high ceilings and a large river rock fireplace as the room's dominant feature. They were seated in oversized sofas covered in a simple cotton fabric. Juliet noticed how the room already gave the impression that it had been lived in for many years. It was furnished in a blend of country antiques and practical pieces. Juliet immediately felt at home. During their cocktails, and while the cassoulet Juliet had cooked was warming up, their conversation ranged from the beauties of the mountains that surrounded them to catching up on the latest news.

Jerry asked Juliet how she had found Southern California, which led to a series of derogatory comments from both Jerry and Justin.

"What I can't understand," said Justin, is how anybody could choose to stay in that hell-hole! The traffic, the rudeness, the crass materialism, all that Hollywood phoniness. Yuk!"

Juliet remained quiet throughout the diatribe.

Jerry chimed in, "Oh, well, I'll never understand people."

Juliet found herself commenting "Come on, guys! Some people don't have the ability to move wherever they wish. Anyway, to Southern Californians, the area is home. Lots of people don't move far from where they were born."

"Well, you can take the smog and the stupid people who choke in it, and stuff them all, I say." Justin commented in a loud and hearty voice.

Juliet felt an unexpected anger rising in her. She could not understand why people were so hateful about California, so prejudiced by what they saw on television. She asked, "O.K., Justin. When was the last time you visited California? Come on, really?"

"Too short a time ago, as far as I'm concerned."

"No, really. Last year? Five years ago? When?" Juliet's flashing eyes underscored her growing anger.

"O.K. About 20 years ago, on a business trip. But I saw enough then to last me a lifetime!" He laughed. "Anyway, why are you acting so defensive? I thought you chose the serenity of the mountains"

Juliet could see his point, but somehow she was still irritated at his generalizations about a place where she had spent most of her adult life.

"You're right in some ways. I love it here. And, sitting in this lovely home, I can easily forget the outside world. That's true. But I guess you ought to know that I have decided to spend some of my time at my other home ... in Southern California. So I guess I'm one of those stupid people!"

There was an awkward silence.

Justin broke the quiet by saying, "I'm sorry. I didn't mean to attack you. I guess we start to live with blinders on in such a protected place."

They went on into dinner, back into a more convivial mood. Juliet still couldn't quiet some of the treacherous thoughts that slipped into her mind about Justin. Why did he feel he had to brag about his choices so much? Why was he judgmental of others' life choices? She remembered now some of their conversations while they were hiking, where they had both extolled the virtues of the Wood River Valley or the Sawtooth Mountains. Juliet had just interpreted them as enthusiasm arising out of the pleasure at the beauties they saw, but now she recalled a smugness in his tone that she had dismissed at the time, not wanting to think it so. She even remembered his assertion that "no mountains in the world are as beautiful as these." At the time she had meant to ask him if he'd ever hiked the Sierra or the Alps but had stifled the challenges as too confrontational.

During dinner Juliet noticed the way Justin ate, greedily, as though he wouldn't get his share. She wondered if his childhood had been as perfect as he had painted it during their long walks.

As a matter of fact, she began to notice things about him that would probably be very irritating if she spent more time with him. At one point Jerry mentioned how he loved to spend hours in the Community Library, again reiterating how fortunate they all were to live in a small town that had such a place, when she heard Justin say, "I don't have time for books. There's too much real life to be lived. Why shut yourself up on beautiful days?"

She felt like retorting, "Why shut off your mind from new ideas?" but didn't. Instead she just stared at him while Jerry carefully explained his justification for the hours he chose to read.

Juliet was reminded of her recalcitrant high school students. She knew with a sudden clarity that, as nice as he might be in other areas of his life, Justin was not a man with whom she needed to spend any more time. She realized that someone with more curiosity was more suitable for her. At the same time, her always-debating mind noted Justin's fine points: he had tons of money, he loved the outdoors, he was handsome, he was certainly eligible, he wanted to be in this town, didn't need to live anywhere else, was involved in environmental causes, did indeed have a practical intelligence. These were certainly plusses. He would make someone a fine mate, she was sure. The truth was, though, that he did wear blinders. He had found a comfortable place in his mind and he chose to stay there. Where was his receptivity to new ideas, his sense of the possibilities of the world and the human spirit? Juliet needed more.

Now Sam, for instance, (she felt the thoughts creeping in) Sam had the openness of mind to see beyond a current moment, an intellectual quest to examine all sides of an issue. It boiled down to the difference between broad and narrow-mindedness.

The rest of the evening passed smoothly, and Juliet was careful to return to her active participation in the evening. While she helped Cassie with the dishes, they settled into comfortable woman-to-woman talk.

"Well?" said Cassie. "What do you think of Justin? I noticed he couldn't keep his eyes off you."

"Oh, Cassie. I think you saw something that wasn't there. I think Justin is just interested in himself, really. He's nice, handsome and all, but I'm probably going to pass on letting this friendship go any further ."

"Shoot." said Cassie, as she put Saran wrap around the leftovers, "Well, it was selfish, I guess. It's just that he and Jerry are friends. You know, not best buddies, but friends. It kind of reminded me of when you and Paul used to be with us."

"I understand, Cassie. But it's not the same. He's not Paul. In fact, he's not Sam. The more I think about it, the more I think you would both really like Sam. He's got a big heart, he's considerate of others' feelings and—well—he's just wonderful!" Juliet reddened at what had come out in this talk. Just as she had decided to spend more time in California, she was reaching the conclusion that she wanted to be with Sam. *If I just let life flow, things fall into place.*

How she would manage her life on two coasts and in Sun Valley all at the same time was something else. Oh well, she decided, I am being a bit premature about all of this. Sam may be thinking that he's well rid of me. Just two more weeks until the BIG phone call.

When they parted at her condominium door and she said "goodnight" to Justin, Juliet could hardly wait to begin writing the letter brewing in her heart.

CHAPTER 20

▼

June 5

Dear Sam

I am beginning this letter a few days before I am supposed to mail it, because I must write down now what is in my heart. It's one-way, I know (or, shall we say the communication is two-way but deferred), but I still feel a need to express myself to you now.

I just returned from an evening with my dearest Idaho friends, Cassie and Jerry. I had dinner at their home and was accompanied by a mutual male friend, Justin Blake. While I have not been "dating" him, we have spent many hours together hiking the mountains of the area, and I have gotten to know him very well. So I know my friends were hoping that maybe a relationship was developing. But tonight at dinner, I missed you. I was polite, and I'm sure the evening was acceptable to everyone else, but I knew that I wanted you to be across the table, not him. So that's what I'm feeling.

But there is more to confess. When I went to California to work on re-renting my home there, I stayed with Barb and Gio until the tenants left. They had a huge beach party on Memorial Day, and there were tons of interesting people and plates loaded with delicious food, and the weather was marvelous, and I was there at one of my favorite places in the whole world, and guess what! I was lonely. Lonely, I realized, without you. And it was <u>you</u> I was thinking about, not the ghosts that have recently intruded on my times with you (even "benevolent" ghosts, like your "benevolent dictators"). I am ready to jump into a relationship with you.

So here's <u>my</u> proposition. Please come meet me in Sun Valley for the Fourth of July weekend. It's great fun here at that time of the year ... rodeos, barbecues, outdoor festivals, all the glories of the "Mountain West." If you book a flight the minute you get this letter, you will still be over the 14 day limit and the tickets won't cost too much (there's that old practicality coming out). I want to start afresh, take the time to really know each other. Every instinct I have tells me that our interests are compatible, and that you are the kind of good man I want in my life.

If you have read this far, you will understand the risk I have decided to take. I will understand if the letter I receive from you is not filled with the same commitment. But I hope so. If not, don't worry. I will be sad, but knowing you has reminded me of the possibilities in this wonderful world. That I could dream of ever caring for someone as I did for Paul is so far beyond my wildest thoughts that I am having trouble absorbing the reality that I do.

Love,
Juliet

Then she took a break for a quick cup of herbal tea and dashed off a note, the one she would mail tomorrow.

June 6

Dear Girls

Thank you for leaving me the address in Australia. I plan to mail this in time for you to receive it before Jen returns to the States. I am thinking of you both, and tonight I am thanking the Powers that Be for the gift of my two lovely girls. I trust you are having a wonderful time together … although, isn't it winter there? Oh well, the sunshine of your souls will light up any gloomy days. (Your mother is still really corny!)

I just wanted you both to know that I did not rent our Santa Monica home. I want it to be available as long as I can possibly afford it, for all of us to visit. I am thrilled at the prospect of having three new sets of keys made, one for each of us, and knowing that anytime anyone of us needs R&R by the ocean, we can have it.

Tasha, Please let me know the exact date of your departure from Thailand. Could you stop in LA and we'll all three meet at 20th Street? I know it's sometime in September, but I'll try to arrange my schedule so I can be there, too. We'll have another time just for the three of us. It's been too long … since Mexico … that we have had just this kind of time together!

I hope I'll have some good news for you by then. (Ha, ha! See? I can still be a woman of mystery!)

I love you both—up to the farthest star in the sky.
Love, Mom

Juliet sealed the letter and put on the Australia address, then poured a hot bath. It was 2:00 a.m. before she closed her eyes, but she fell asleep with more peace than she could remember feeling in many years. She dreamed of clear, empty beaches and sunsets on the horizon.

*   *   *   *

Sam … I'm adding this to the letter I started on the 5th. I almost threw it away in a random act of cowardice, but I have decided to damn the torpedoes and hope that you are receptive to my emotions.

I'm going to try to stop analyzing my feelings and worrying things to death. I hope that I can learn to be more spontaneous. Perhaps you can help me with this aspect of my character—the stubborn refusal to relax and just let life happen. In a way, that's what I am doing now, so maybe this is a start. I am going to let this thing we've started take its course.

I await the arrival of your letter. I promise you I will not open it until the 15th.

I assume that shortly after you read this I will be hearing from you. (Cheers to two-way communication!)

Goodbye for now,

Love, Juliet

*   *   *   *

It was 6:30 on June 15, and Juliet could hardly retain her composure, with the mixture of apprehension and excitement churning within. She went downstairs to her bedroom, fluffed up the pillows, and picked up the crossword puzzle she was midway through. In five minutes she was calmed down a bit. She had always found that diving into the *New York Times* puzzle could distract her from more pressing concerns. Now, as she tried to fathom this particular week's theme/challenge, she could not obsess about the phone ringing or not ringing.

Just before 7:00, she took Sam's letter from the nightstand where she had carefully placed it the night before and opened it.

June 10

My dearest Juliet

Here goes. I hope that your letter to me will contain at least part of the positive feelings I am putting into mine. Since we talked, I have picked up a pen or the telephone several times, wanting to cancel our arrangement and wanting to talk to you. This waiting period has been very difficult—atrocious, in fact—for all I want to do is hear your voice and tell you that I understand everything about Paris and what happened, and that I want us to continue this relationship. In short, I have missed you terribly!

So I am risking another rejection when I write you this letter. You may very well have decided to terminate our friendship. After all, you are a woman who has found a new life and deserves to be with someone who lives nearby, at the very least. I am in the depths of New Hampshire and still involved with my teaching, for at least a few years more. My life is here, yours is there. I know you are practical, and I do think that you might have second thoughts about a long-distance relationship. And, then, there is the risk that all the connections we have made are too uncomfortable to you. I respect that, if it is so.

Or, finally, you just may not be all that attracted to me.

At any rate, the purpose of this letter is to let you know about my conclusions during this period of re-thinking. I have come to the realization that I want you in my life and will do anything to make that so.

So there! It's said and done. I hope you feel the same.

By the way, I saw Elise again last weekend. As I held her dear little body in my arms, I could only think how much I wanted you there to be able to understand the sense of renewal and joy it gave me.

I think we both deserve a renewal of life with each other.

Love, Sam.

When the phone rang at exactly 7:00, it came almost as a surprise, and Juliet sensed the adrenaline pumping through her system. She picked it up.

"Hi, Sam."

"Juliet." There was a lengthy pause. "Did my letter arrive on time?"

"It came just yesterday. But I was a good girl. I just now opened it."

"Yours got here yesterday, too. It took all of my childhood Boy Scouts' honors not to peek at it, but I did the honorable thing and waited."

"So? What did you think?" By now Juliet could almost think her beating heart was sounding out for him to hear.

"Well, you've read mine, so you should know. All I can say is I wish I were there to take you in my arms."

"Oh?" Juliet's voice faltered.

"Yes. And Yes to the Fourth of July. And Yes to all that implies. I already booked my flight to Sun Valley."

"Oh, Sam. Thank god. When I got your letter I was afraid to open it, afraid that in reflection you would reconsider. I wouldn't have blamed you."

"While we're on that subject, can we start anew here? Let's cancel Paris and your nightmares and have no more recriminations, O.K?"

"O.K. Oh, Sam, how am I so lucky?"

"Funny, I was just going to say the same thing. You realize, don't you, that the truth is that both of us are entitled to happiness, or at least to a second chance? It doesn't matter what our lives were before, and, by the way, I think we both were part of good relationships where we honored our mates and were faithful to our vows. If anything, your long and happy marriage to Paul makes you more attractive to me. I know that you have the qualities I want, that you'll wear well, for example."

"You make me sound like a carpet or a washing machine!" Juliet laughed.

"That wasn't well-phrased, but I know you know what I mean. Again Sam paused. "I love you, Juliet."

"Oh, Sam. I can't believe all of this."

"Yes, you can. I'm a serious man, in many ways. I understand the force of words. I wouldn't say that unless I meant it."

Suddenly she was shivering. Juliet pulled up the afghan throw Nana had made and wrapped it around her.

"I believe you. Now what, Sam? When do you plan on arriving? How much time can you spend?"

"I hope you don't mind that I took the liberty of booking a flight to arrive July 3 and then return July 14 (Bastille Day)——ten days out there. After I finished the book, I find myself with spare time."

"Wonderful. I hoped you would be here for at least that long."

They continued to make plans for his visit and then, as she said goodbye, Juliet heard herself saying, "Take care. I love you, Sam."

She realized after she had hung up that she had voiced the words she had been thinking.

Juliet picked up the letter and read over and over again the lines about Sam wanting her in his life. She would have to make some changes as well, she knew, if they were to spend good amounts of time together. Well, that was something they would discuss over the Fourth.

She wanted to share her good news. She again felt like a schoolgirl after the prom. Her beau had danced beautifully with her, though over telephone lines instead of on a dance floor. She was left with the need to keep the memory alive by telling someone about it.

Finally, she dialed Barb's number and was thrilled when she heard her friend's husky voice.

"Barb, oh, Barb! Hi! It's Juliet. I have to share something with you!" She found herself tumbling over her words as she spilled out everything to her friend. How they had made the pact to wait to write the letters, what she had felt, all the frustrations and fears of the past few weeks jumbled together in her torrent of words as she spilled out all her emotions to her friend.

When she finished, Barbara was laughing on the other end of the phone. Juliet could almost see her smiling. "So, my friend. You've rejoined the world of the living. It's about time for your reawakening! Gio's not home now, but I can't wait to tell him. I know he'll be as happy as I am for you."

They chatted for awhile longer, vowing to see each other as soon as possible.

Juliet returned to the crossword puzzle and then a good book, willing the hours away until it was time to sleep. At last she was able to still the restlessness of her soul, but she did one other thing before turning out the lights. She placed Sam's letter under her pillow in homage to a youthful superstition. Whenever she had been to weddings she kept a sliver of the cake to go under her pillow. Her mother had told her she would dream that night of the man she would marry if she did so. Thank goodness most of the men she fancied at that young age did not materialize. She couldn't remember now whether she had ever dreamt of Paul over wedding cake. So when she put Sam's letter under her pillow, she was glad no one could see her do so. It was foolish and childish. But somehow it felt all right, this magical evening, to escape into girlish imaginings. This dream might come true.

CHAPTER 21

▼

Juliet finished watering the pots of geraniums, petunias and pansies on her deck, dusted the outdoor furniture, went back in the house to check its appearance and then noticed that she had half an hour left before Sam's flight was due.

She put Spanky into the Jeep and drove through weekend traffic to the airport in Hailey, 12 miles from her doorstep. Even the stretch of highway seemed festive, matching the area's profusion of flags. Bikers and roller-bladers swept along the bike path which for the most part paralleled the thoroughfare, giving the view the flavor of people enjoying themselves. The path also had walkers, babies in bike strollers, and dogs on leashes. The gaiety Juliet felt was matched by those around her.

Spanky had his nose out the rear seat window left slightly ajar for this purpose. In his doggy way, he, too, was happy, Juliet thought. What could be better than a hot summer day, the chance to be outside, the promise of a long span of time till darkness descended, maybe about 9:30 or so, and being with someone you love? Both she and Spanky shared these bountiful conditions!

This time, when she saw the lanky figure emerge from the airplane, Juliet had no doubts about his identity. He was just the man she wanted to see, and she clung to him through the short wait for baggage and all the way to her car. When Sam got in, she noticed that he already seemed to belong here, next to her. He wore khakis and a blazer, probably more formal for this area than he would need to be, but his tanned face and deep voice just fit, somehow.

When they arrived at her home, she felt slightly awkward giving him the tour of the house, but they both felt more comfortable when they took a few minutes to sit on her deck and enjoy the afternoon sun and iced tea. Juliet had put Ella Fitzgerald on the CD player.

They chatted about everything that had happened since Paris, avoiding any mention of their emotions.

"O.K. Grandpa's prerogative." Sam said, as he took out his wallet and a section with pictures of Elise. "This one was taken only minutes after her birth, but this one's better, don't you think? I just got it from Matthew a couple of days ago. She's seven weeks old here."

Juliet couldn't stop smiling, "oohing and ahing" over the photos. "Is her hair the color in this picture? It looks red!"

"I think she may wind up with red hair. Betsy's aunt had bright red hair."

Juliet realized they hadn't mentioned either Paul or Betsy's names yet. She took the opportunity to bring something up she'd had on her mind. "Speaking of Betsy and your family," she said, "Do they know you're here? How do they feel about it?"

"Yes, I told them. Funny thing is, Michael is 100% behind the notion of our being together. I would have thought that he would be the one less enthusiastic, as he lives with me and sees me all the time. But he even cited studies he'd come across in the medical library showing that widowers who remarry sooner rather than later have a longer life span. He says it's because we're so used to having a good woman in our life that we just naturally want another."

Juliet ignored the reference to marriage. "I've heard the same thing, but in my case, it's that widows often thrive after their mates are gone. They get chances to do things they've always wanted to, you know, spread their wings, etc. But then, after awhile, most women opt for remarriage, (*oops, there's that word again*) if there's a chance. But of course, the odds are less … so many available women, so few good men the older you get." Juliet put her hand on her forehead to shade her eyes from the bright afternoon sun so she could see Sam better. Ella was singing "Someone to Watch Over Me."

She arose to refill their glasses. When she returned, Ella was finishing the lyrics.

"Were you listening to that?" she said, putting two frosty glasses down on the patio table.

"Sure was. What timing! Is that what we really all want? Someone to watch over us?"

"I don't know. But you know what?" Juliet said, leaning over and taking his free hand across the table. "I don't care anymore about my motives. I think I'm learning to enjoy what is offered me." They both stayed quiet for a long few seconds until Juliet broke the silence. "So, you just said that Michael was O.K. about us. Implied in that was a thought that perhaps Matthew and Cindy aren't."

"I really can't say. I'm not sure how they feel. They are so caught up right now with new parenthood, and they talk a lot about how much they wish Betsy were able to enjoy her grand-daughter. They don't mention you. I guess I interpret that as less than an endorsement, but maybe I'm being unfair. I did tell them I was coming to Sun Valley for the Fourth, as they had wanted me to come to Maine. I don't know if their disappointment was over Grandpa not being there or over my increased involvement with you."

"Well, they were unfailingly polite to me in New Hampshire. I think they've done well, considering. I can imagine that it is hard for any adult child to see his parent with someone else, especially if their folks had a good relationship." She watched a group of putters taking their time with the lie of the green. "Maybe its like golf. They are waiting until they have a clearer sense of the landscape before they decide to give it their all, to focus in. Maybe they think I'm a transition person. Could be."

"They're wrong, then. I'm not searching for anyone else."

Juliet couldn't talk. Her throat was constricted.

Sam looked closely at her, squeezing her hand. "My. My. What I'm saying, what I'm doing. It feels right to me. Eventually it will feel right to my kids, I know. But you haven't told me about yours."

"As you know, they've both just returned from their vacation together. Jen and I have talked a lot about how well Tasha is doing, what a grand time they had together, and so forth. But we've not gotten around to what is going on in my life. I thought I'd wait until our time here together was over and then tell them what's up. I don't want them to get too involved. They do know you're here. When I call Jen tomorrow, I hope you'll have chance to talk with her."

Sam arose and stretched. "Would you mind if I took a shower and cleaned up a bit?

"Of course. Oh. And when you change, just be casual. We're going to a rodeo tonight."

"Guess I am in the West, Ma'am," Sam said. "Which bathroom do you want me to use?"

"Mine, of course. There's plenty of room, double sinks, and the shower is much better than the one in the guest bathroom. I also left you space in the closet and the two top drawers of the tall bureau. While you're showering, I'll finish up our picnic dinner."

To her chagrin, Juliet wasn't able to look Sam in the eyes while giving him these directions. So she was still shy!

✳　　✳　　✳　　✳

The rodeo arena may not have been the best place for Juliet's picnic fare, but they arrived early enough to avoid the worst traffic and to be able to eat cold Chinese chicken salad and crunchy Ciabatta bread without too many interruptions as people took their seats. Sam enjoyed the rodeo immensely, and when the fireworks show following the last event lit up the sky, she imagined she could see the little boy within him. They kept saying "Oh gosh, Wow" and other childlike exclamations; they couldn't control the excitement and wonder.

On the way home, Sam said, "What a neat thing to do! I haven't been to a rodeo since I was about 10 and my dad took me to one in Madison Square Garden. I felt like a kid again!"

"I was looking at you and thinking that exact thing ... that I could picture you as a child. I've never even asked you about your childhood. Where were you born?"

"Actually, Syracuse. My dad was a pharmacist, so I hung out a lot around his drugstore. I always thought I'd want to do the same. It skipped a generation, though, the real dedication to the kind of scientific studies that Matthew has had."

The rest of the trip home, they reminisced about their respective childhoods, often touching and laughing.

As they came in through the front door, they were still smiling from one of Sam's anecdotes. It wasn't until they took off their jackets that a moment of silence passed. Juliet looked up at the suddenly serious and hungry expression on Sam's face, felt her own desire stir, and led him to her bedroom. This time she had no nightmares.

*   *   *   *

Juliet awoke before Sam, took a quick shower and put on some tights and a t-shirt before going upstairs to the kitchen. She heard the coffee finish its brewing cycle as Sam came into the kitchen. He sat down on one of the stools by the counter, and Juliet gave him a steaming cup of coffee.

"Did you sleep well?" he asked, inhaling the fragrance of the coffee.

"Very well. How about you?"

"Wonderfully." Juliet sat down on the stool next to him and they both looked out the window above the sink at the line of mountains reflecting the morning sun.

"This is one of the purely great moments of life," Sam said, as Juliet turned her attention towards him, "sitting here with a delicious cup of coffee, looking out at the mountains, next to someone I love. What could be better?"

Spanky nuzzled his leg. "Oh, and excuse me, I need to add, and with a fabulous dog to pet." He stroked Spanky's head.

Juliet smiled. "I know what you mean. All's right with the world."

As Juliet arose to refill their cups, she said, "How about breakfast on the deck? We don't have that many days in the year when we can do that, but I think today's one of them." She checked the thermometer she kept hanging outside of the kitchen window. "It's already 70 ... probably means a scorcher for Idaho."

"Sure, but only if you let me fix breakfast. I told you I knew how to cook, so let me show you."

So while Juliet followed him around the kitchen, pointing out the location of all the utensils and cooking gear, Sam prepared omelettes studded with some of the fresh produce Juliet had purchased from the farmers' market. Onions, mushrooms, green peppers, an avocado, home-grown tomatoes, and grated Idaho spuds filled the fluffy eggs. They took their plates to the patio and Juliet found herself wolfing down the delicious concoction.

'My gosh! You weren't kidding, were you. You're hired."

"Am I, really?" Sam said the words slowly, and again Juliet experienced the stomach-crunch of desire.

Denying her rush of emotion, Juliet sipped more coffee, then said, "Think you could also serve as my nightmare-banisher? How does that sound? 'Wanted: cook, nightmare-banisher and all around wonderful man to brighten the life of formerly lonely widow. Stupid men need not apply'."

"Sounds good to me. Where do I fill out the application?"

"Right here." Juliet got up, went over to Sam's chair and kissed him for along time in full view of early golfers. She didn't care.

When they stopped the embrace, Sam got up and led her gently down stairs where they again made love. Afterwards, he said, "You see? I am a young boy again. Rejuvenated and ready to take on life. Thank you, my darling."

Only later did Juliet realize that they had left the dishes, crusted with egg remnants, on the table. Never in her life had she not cleared the table before doing anything else.

*   *   *   *

They had been invited to a picnic at Redfish Lake with Cassie and Jerry. Usually Juliet would have avoided the crowds that generally flocked to this nearby lake for camping over the long holiday, but she didn't care. She felt she could endure any discomfort or delay if Sam were by her side. They decided to go in their own car so they could stop along the way, and Juliet enjoyed being able to point out the things she loved about this magnificent part of the world. As they drove over Galena Summit, she noted the history of the region, how ore wagons had once pulled their loads over this very spot, how sheep had traversed these ranges. She loved the mix of mining and sheep and cattle ranching, the still visible ghost towns, the presence of wildlife even close to the homes sprouting up everywhere.

They stopped the Jeep at the summit's lookout, and Juliet pointed out the mouth of the Salmon River and the mountains of the Sawtooth Range, so aptly named for its snaggle-toothed appearance. By the time they arrived at the picnic spot Cassie and Jerry occupied, her throat was hoarse.

As she introduced Sam to Cassie and Jerry, she noticed that the two men were immediately at ease with each other. She needn't have worried about not being with Justin. Good friends always accepted those loved by their friends.

They spent the afternoon hiking the trails at the west end of the lake and then returned to their spot close to the sandy stretch of beach now filled with families barbecuing hot dogs and lighting sparklers.

"Let's take a quick swim before it starts to get cold," Cassie suggested, removing her t-shirt and shorts to show her firm, tan body in a swimsuit. This was one of those times Juliet had dreaded, the full impact of her age being revealed, but she quickly did the same, and the two women ran to the cold water and dove in. The men followed suit, and soon all four were swimming and splashing. Jerry got out after a few minutes and put air in two small floating rafts. He brought them to Juliet and Cassie, who thanked him and then hopped on, paddling out to the farthest buoys.

"What fun!" Cassie said, turning her head to watch Juliet, almost asleep on the float.

"I agree. I can't remember when I've enjoyed being silly so much. Reminds me of the times when I was a teenager and my girlfriend Darlene and I would go to Lake Tahoe with her family during the summers. We'd take *True Romance Magazine* out on floats with us and read the good parts to each other. Her dad would have exploded if he'd caught us. Almost did, the time my float sprung a leak and he came out to rescue me!"

They both laughed.

"Actually, Cassie. I'm a bit scared. It's too wonderful right now. Do you ever have that feeling? When life is going so well, that somehow you don't deserve it and that something awful will happen to snatch it away from you?"

"The truth? No, I don't feel that way at all. I just try to enjoy the good times. That's my reward for getting through the bad times."

"I wish I could do that. My friend who is in AA says they have an expression, 'This too shall pass.' That means that bad times will eventually go away, but the reverse is that so will the good times."

"I think that's too pat an idea. There is no reason we can't decide to enjoy life to the fullest. I don't mean that we can ignore tragedies and the sadness of life, but that when we have a chance, we just have to grab the brass ring, to use another cliché."

"Actually, that's what AA teaches, too. And it's what I really, really, try to believe. I just can't seem to get rid of the vestige of some Puritanical concept that enjoyment and pleasure are somehow not deserved, are sinful." Juliet splashed water on her friend, who had now paddled up next to her. "But I'm trying. Oh, how I'm trying!"

Cassie splashed her back. "Spoken like a woman in love. Are you?"

"Yep!" said Juliet, as she and Cassie began a hearty water fight that resulted in both of them falling off their rafts and finally swimming back to shore, floats in tow.

*   *   *   *

The next week passed by as a dream, a haze of food and wine and love and long walks, reading good books, talking all the time, tennis and picnics and friends over for dinner. The day before Sam was to return to New Hampshire, they went on a three-hour hike up to the Pioneer Cabin. They had taken the "long way" which led them through and around steep passes and ravines before they eventually reached the small log cabin where people could spend the night or rest before the two-hour-or-so hike back down the mountain. They hadn't tried to hike hurriedly, instead stopping frequently to note the scenery or the have a sip of water from their canteens. Juliet thought the day perfect, but when they returned to the condo, Sam suggested that they rest awhile and then shower and get dressed up for dinner.

When Juliet mentioned that she had some fish for dinner, he demurred, saying he had decided on a special place.

Juliet found herself getting into a dress for the first time in two weeks. As she applied the final touches of mascara and lipstick, she noted with a twinge of vanity, that she looked more tanned and fit than she had in years. Even with sunscreen, the high-altitude reflection of the sun had bronzed her cheeks. She had shed a couple of pounds and enjoyed the feeling of the loose belt at her waist. She was ready to celebrate!

Sam insisted on driving this night. They were on a date, he said, so he wanted to treat her appropriately. He continued this thread as he opened the doors for her and waited until she was seated at the corner table of one of her favorite restaurants in town, Felix.

On the table, in addition to the display of flowers on all the tables, were a dozen fresh red roses, hued with the same brilliant shade as were the crystal earrings from Paris. Juliet had worn them for the occasion, a fortuitous thing, she thought.

The waiter immediately brought them champagne. As he filled their glasses, Juliet kept her eyes locked on Sam's. They were gleaming with anticipation. She caught the mood.

"I guess I am being courted. Certainly feels like it, and I love it!" As Sam reached across the table and took her hand, they both picked up their fluted glasses and clicked them.

"To the most lovely woman in the world." Sam said, as they toasted.

"Thank you Sam." Those were the only words Juliet could find, as garrulous as she might normally be. She was once again feeling giddy, but not from the champagne.

They ordered starters of calamari, exquisite salads with fine tiny raspberries in season as a garnish, then main courses of salmon and lamb cooked to perfection. Juliet hardly touched the wine, preferring to keep all her senses intact for the evening.

For dessert, they were served crème brulees and espresso. Normally, Juliet wouldn't indulge in caffeine at this late hour, but she didn't care if she ever slept again. She didn't want this evening to stop.

As they sipped the rich coffee and looked out the window, the sunset was touching the tips of the mountains in their view. The glow lit up the clear sky and seemed to surround them. They were both quiet, taking in the beauty before them.

Finally, Sam said. "Do you remember the first morning after I arrived and you said you might hire me as your nightmare-banisher, among other things? I want to tell you a little story that has kept coming into my mind these past several days."

The waiter came over to refill their glasses with fresh water. Sam took a sip and continued, "When the boys were little, one of their favorite books was called *There's a Nightmare in my Closet*. It's a brief story about a little guy who goes to bed every night afraid of the monster he imagines is hiding in his closet. Finally, one night the monster comes out, and the little boy invites him to come into bed with him. They become great pals sharing their evenings together. As the book ends, they are cuddled together imagining another threatening nightmare in the closet."

Juliet smiled. She heard in his voice all the tenderness he must have shown as a father to his two sons. She loved him more this minute than she ever had.

He continued, "Well, when you told me after Paris about your nightmare, my first reaction was that I could have cuddled with you and driven the demons away. But being with you this week I have given that idea a different spin. You see, I do think you have nightmares in your closet. I have them, too. But I think we can, indeed, huddle together and take comfort in loving each other if we invite those nightmares to come to bed with us. In other words, if we just accept that there will always be those as you put it, "benevolent" nightmares, we can live with them. We don't need to be afraid of them anymore. We don't have to be afraid of anything, ever again"

Juliet held his hand again and hoped to press his spirit even more firmly into hers.

"So, I'm signing up for the job you wanted me to do. Juliet, my love, will you share my bed and put to rest your fears and bad dreams and marry me?"

He took out a tiny box from his pocket and passed it cross the table to her. The sun went down and the candles now glowed even more fully on her face. She opened the box and saw a simple band of blood-red rubies and diamonds.

"Yes," was all she said. *Yes.*

CHAPTER 22

▼

The frigid air was thin and brittle, signaling the start of a cold snap. Juliet wore her heavy black full-length coat, a muffler, lined mittens and a double-knit cap, and still she felt the chill of Idaho's December. Tourists struggled with packages and groceries, ski racks held multiple pairs of skis on top of rented Explorers and Blazers. Ketchum had a festive air, the mood of a tourist town with lots of visitors and the resultant sound of cash registers and peoples' laughter filling the crowded shops.

But Juliet shivered in the crisp air. Luckily, Tash and Jen were at her side as others began to gather around the tree for the annual hospice lighting ceremony, their breaths combined in thick bursts of fog as they spoke. In spite of the discomfort of cold she felt, she knew that she would never miss one of these rituals; as long as she spent the season in the Wood River Valley, she would honor those who could no longer be here by contributing to the hospice and lighting a candle.

Her daughters, one on each side of her, encircled her with their arms and held each other's hands in the process. The ceremony began, first with the singing of carols and then the naming of the departed. Again Juliet noted the faces of those grieving, those now reconciled to their losses, those who helped their own recoveries by assisting others. She was one of the first to hear a familiar name.

"Barnes, Paul Barnes."

Jen and Tasha went over to the tree, lit two candles, and placed them on the closest boughs. Juliet closed her eyes after she saw that the girls had completed their homage to Paul. She said a silent prayer to the memory of her late husband: *Paul:, I pray you are safe and warm in another life. I will always thank you for the life you gave me and our girls. I love you.* She felt the warmth of arms around her again, opened her eyes and, seeing Sam's big fleece-jacketed arms around her waist, turned around to lean into his embrace. Jen and Tash returned and stood next to Sam, the threesome as close as possible. When the name "Duncan, Betsy Duncan," was called, Sam stepped forward to honor her. Now the threesome was Juliet and her daughters. As Sam returned to their side, the girls embraced him.

When the naming of names was over and the large fir glittered with the real candles and the artificial lights, spreading its healing message through the town, those gathered around it joined in the final carol, as in past years singing "Silent Night." Juliet looked at her dear family: Jen, showing a maturity, sweetness, and spirit that her mother would always admire, Tasha, full of confidence combined with a loving concern for others, the kind of compassion that would be rewarded by warm and caring relationships, and Sam, his Sam-Paul face now streaked with tears. While tears also filled her eyes, Juliet was able to recognize that her deep hurt was settled, somehow put in its proper niche in her soul. She had this night and the rest of her life to accept the beauty and love that lay ahead.

The four of them walked around the corner, got into her Jeep and headed home together.

978-0-595-51720-6
0-595-51720-X

Printed in the United States
123736LV00002B/127-174/P